W9-AHG-750

"I won't live with you before we're married." Her lips pressed together in a line.

Donovan was suddenly hit with the urge to kiss the tightness away.

No, that wouldn't do. This was business, not pleasure. He had to remember that.

"Sarah, be rational. Since we're not sharing a bedroom, even after we're married, it doesn't matter when you move in. It's not as if I'm planning to ravish you."

He wasn't planning to, but that didn't stop him from fantasizing about it. Ravishing Sarah was something he hadn't completely been able to put out of his mind. During the daytime he was able to relegate the thought to the recesses of his awareness, but at night...

His dreams about her had nothing to do with a platonic business arrangement....

Dear Reader,

Spend your rainy March days with us! Put on a pot of tea (or some iced tea if you're in that mood), grab a snuggly blanket and settle in for a day of head-to-toe-warming—guaranteed by reading a Silhouette Romance novel!

Seeing double lately? This month's twin treats include *Her Secret Children* (#1648) by Judith McWilliams, in which our heroine discovers her frozen eggs have been stolen—and falls for her babies' father! Then, in Susan Meier's *The Tycoon's Double Trouble* (#1650), her second DAYCARE DADS title, widower Troy Cramer gets help raising his precocious daughters from an officer of the law—who also threatens his heart....

You might think of giving your heart a workout with some of our other Romance titles. In *Protecting the Princess* (#1649) by Patricia Forsythe, a bodyguard gets a royal makeover when he poses as the princess's fiancé. Meanwhile, the hero of Cynthia Rutledge's *Kiss Me, Kaitlyn* (#1651) undergoes a "make*under*" to conceal he's the company's wealthy boss. In Holly Jacobs's *A Day Late and a Bride Short* (#1653), a fake engagement starts feeling like the real thing. And while the marriage isn't pretend in Sue Swift's *In the Sheikh's Arms* (#1652), the hero never intended to fall in love, not when the union was for revenge!

Be sure to come back next month for more emotion-filled love stories from Silhouette Romance. I know I can't wait!

Mary-Theresa Hussey

Mary-Theresa Hussey
Senior Editor

Please address questions and book requests to:
Silhouette Reader Service
U.S.: 3010 Walden Ave., P.O. Box 1325, Buffalo, NY 14269
Canadian: P.O. Box 609, Fort Erie, Ont. L2A 5X3

A Day Late and a Bride Short

HOLLY JACOBS

*Barb,
It was so great
finally meeting you.
~ Holly
7/05*

SILHOUETTE **Romance**®

Published by Silhouette Books

America's Publisher of Contemporary Romance

If you purchased this book without a cover you should be aware that this book is stolen property. It was reported as "unsold and destroyed" to the publisher, and neither the author nor the publisher has received any payment for this "stripped book."

To Cheryl (Ludwig) St.John, a woman who's inspired me and always provided a shoulder to lean on. I started out her fan and—though I still am one of her biggest—I'm honored to call her friend, as well.

Special thanks to Chris Trejchel, attorney extraordinaire, for his legalese help. And to his wife, Cathy, for marrying well and providing me with a great resource!

 SILHOUETTE BOOKS

ISBN 0-373-19653-9

A DAY LATE AND A BRIDE SHORT

Copyright © 2003 by Holly Fuhrmann

All rights reserved. Except for use in any review, the reproduction or utilization of this work in whole or in part in any form by any electronic, mechanical or other means, now known or hereafter invented, including xerography, photocopying and recording, or in any information storage or retrieval system, is forbidden without the written permission of the editorial office, Silhouette Books, 300 East 42nd Street, New York, NY 10017 U.S.A.

All characters in this book have no existence outside the imagination of the author and have no relation whatsoever to anyone bearing the same name or names. They are not even distantly inspired by any individual known or unknown to the author, and all incidents are pure invention.

This edition published by arrangement with Harlequin Books S.A.

® and TM are trademarks of Harlequin Books S.A., used under license. Trademarks indicated with ® are registered in the United States Patent and Trademark Office, the Canadian Trade Marks Office and in other countries.

Visit Silhouette at www.eHarlequin.com

Printed in U.S.A.

Books by Holly Jacobs

Silhouette Romance

Do You Hear What I Hear? #1557
A Day Late and a Bride Short #1653

HOLLY JACOBS

can't remember a time when she didn't read...and read a lot. Writing her own stories just seemed a natural outgrowth of that love. Reading, writing, chauffeuring kids to and from activities makes for a busy life. But it's one she wouldn't trade for any other.

Holly lives in Erie, Pennsylvania, with her husband, four children and a one-hundred-and-eighty-pound Old English mastiff. In her "spare" time, Holly loves hearing from her fans. You can write to her at P.O. Box 11102, Erie, PA 16514-1102.

Dear Reader,

With *A Day Late and a Bride Short,* I am bringing you back to Erie's Perry Square business district. I thought I'd use this Dear Reader letter to apologize to all the real businesses in the real Perry Square. You're all wonderful! But for the purposes of these books, I've reinvented the square. In *Do You Hear What I Hear?* I added Snips and Snaps Beauty Salon and Gardner's Ophthalmology. With this book you'll find Wagner, McDuffy and Chambers Law Firm, and By Design, my heroine's new decorating business. Yes, I'm crowding out the real businesses on the square, but if you're ever in Erie, I hope you look them up! And if you're ever here, I hope you enjoy the view of our bay as much as this book's heroine, Sarah, does. I'll confess, I mention the bay, Lake Erie and Presque Isle a lot in my books because I love them all. (No, the city isn't giving me a tourism kickback!) There's nothing more satisfying than sitting at the water's edge and just watching life go by, or watching the boats sail past and the seagulls glide, or the sun set, or… Well, the only thing that could be better is reading a romance!

Okay, I've plugged my favorite city, my favorite lake and my favorite genre. I think it's about time to end this letter. I hope you enjoy Sarah and Donovan's story. Please feel free to write me (I love to hear from readers!) at www.HollysBooks.com, or by sending me mail at P.O. Box 11102, Erie, PA 16514-1102. Thanks so much and happy reading!

Holly Jacobs

Chapter One

"I feel I'm partner material," Elias Donovan said. He sat, back ramrod straight, every coal-black hair in place and his dark green eyes meeting the firm's senior partner's, Leland Wagner.

This was it. Donovan had everything in place. It was time to lay it on the line.

He began to verbally run through his mental checklist. "I've been with the firm for six years, and I've generated more income for you than any other associate. I have a solid client base and—"

"Elias..."

Donovan winced at the sound of his first name. Leland was one of the few people he permitted to use it. *Elias* sounded too soft, and Donovan wasn't the least bit soft. He'd spent years perfecting his rock-hard court persona, and the name Donovan suited it to a T.

"...we're all aware of what an asset you are to the firm. You're promising partner material and we all realize it."

"Promising?" Donovan asked.

He didn't like the sound of being *promising*. He carefully schooled his expression so his displeasure didn't show.

"You've accomplished everything you just mentioned and more. The only concern we have, Elias, is your lack of balance. You've got work and...? What else is there in your life?" he asked.

As senior partner of Wagner, McDuffy and Chambers, Leland Wagner seemed to feel as if he had to play father to the entire firm. Or maybe it wasn't that he was senior partner, but that he had reached an age where he could have been father, or even grandfather, to all the associates and employees of the firm.

"Work is my life," Donovan said.

Work was his passion, and like any mistress, she was jealous of time he spent elsewhere. Donovan was happy to indulge her. He found his relationship with his practice was so much more straightforward than any relationship he'd ever had with a woman. The law he could understand, but he'd never totally figured out the female species. And he'd given up trying to figure them out at least for now. The day would come that he'd be ready to settle down, but it wasn't here yet.

"Work's not enough," Leland said. "I've been in this business for my entire adult life—over four decades—and it's not enough. It might not be politically correct to say, but you need someone to come home to. You need the balance of a life outside the firm and the courthouse. You need a wife. When we see that you've learned that there's more to life than your practice, then it will be time to talk about partnership."

"A wife?" Donovan echoed. He'd never even dated the same woman for more than a few months. Why would Leland think he was interested in tying his life to one?

"A wife," Leland repeated gently. "I know you think this is an archaic idea. But Dorothy and I are celebrating our fiftieth wedding anniversary next week. I married her right out of high school and she's been my balance all these years. She's my reason for going home at night. She's—"

Donovan interrupted. "How about a fiancée?"

He heard the words come out of his mouth, but couldn't believe he was saying them. *A fiancée?* He didn't have a fiancée. He didn't want a fiancée any more than he wanted a wife.

"A fiancée?" Leland echoed, as if he could hear Donovan's thoughts.

Thinking fast on his feet, Donovan said, "I know

she's not quite a wife, at least not yet, but you're right, she's given my life balance. I can hardly remember a time without her.''

Leland's eyes narrowed as he studied Donovan. ''When did this happen?''

Feeling rather like a teenager lying about the dent in the car, he said, ''Recently.'' That wasn't quite a lie. He'd acquired a fiancée about two seconds ago.

''Well,'' Leland said slowly. A smile suddenly blossomed on his life-lined face. ''You certainly do keep things close to your chest, my boy. That's what makes you such a great lawyer.''

The older man paused a moment and then repeated, ''A fiancée? This puts an entirely different spin on the matter. I'll talk to the other partners, but in the meantime you had better bring her along to the party next week so we can all meet her. I'm sure everyone will want to meet the woman who finally melted the legendary Iceman. You're a private man, Elias. I can respect that, but Wagner, McDuffy and Chambers is a family. And if she's marrying you, she'll be part of that family. So you just bring her and introduce her around.''

''I will,'' he found himself promising.

''Like I said, I'll talk to the other partners, and get back to you with our decision soon.'' Leland stood.

Donovan followed suit, and extended his hand. ''Thank you, Leland.''

Donovan walked out of the office with a sinking

feeling in the pit of his stomach. He couldn't decide if he'd just made things better or worse. But either way, he had something to take care of and there was no time to waste.

Elias Donovan had to find a fiancée…fast.

Sarah Jane Madison took a deep breath. This was it. Her last hope. If this didn't work—

She refused to think about it. This would work. It had to.

"Hi, Amelia." She occasionally met the chatty receptionist in the park for lunch and genuinely liked the woman. She had spiky blond hair, piercing blue eyes that always sparkled with a hint of laughter, and an infectious grin. Add all that to her gregarious personality and it would be next to impossible not to like her.

"Donovan's expecting you. You've got the cream of the crop. At least the cream of the single bachelor crop here at Wagner, McDuffy and Chambers. He's just at top of the stairs, to the right. You can't miss it. I'm sure he's the lawyer here to take care of *all your needs*." Amelia winked and shot Sarah a wicked grin.

Sarah laughed. "If he can take care of my legal problems, he'll have satisfied every one of my needs for him."

"Well, I could think of a few needs of my own for him. Tall, dark and handsome—" Amelia sounded practically ready to swoon ''—and those green eyes. Why sometimes I swear he can look right into my very soul. But the feeling never lasts. He never gives up a single emotion.''

Amelia paused then added, ''On second thought, don't need him too much. Stick to needing him for legal matters. He's the sort of man who uses women up. Not that he's mean, or anything. He's just cold. And a woman can only stand a cold man for so long and then something inside her freezes as well. I don't want to see that happen to you.''

''It's not going to happen because the only thing I need Elias Donovan for is his legal expertise. Nothing more, nothing less.''

''Fine.'' Amelia didn't look convinced, but she headed toward the front door. ''Up the stairs and to the right. I'll talk to you tomorrow.''

Sarah started up the long, marble staircase. Wagner, McDuffy and Chambers had a beautiful building, though it could use a little sprucing up. She'd replace those heavy blinds and let in some more light. And some of the furniture didn't fit the stately grace of the building. She'd—

Sarah stopped herself. She wasn't here to redecorate the building, she was here to get some legal advice.

She reached Donovan's door and knocked.

''Come in.''

She opened the door, expecting something in line

with the outer office area. Instead, what she found was clutter.

Piles of paper, files, boxes of who-knew-what. The walls were white, and there were functional department store blinds on the windows. That was it. No pictures on the walls, nothing personal at all. The office was devoid of any indication of who its inhabitant was. She stood taking in the room until Donovan cleared his throat.

"Miss Madison." He gave a nod. "You said you needed to see me right away?"

Sarah shifted nervously from foot to foot. "I do. I appreciate you seeing me so fast."

"Anything for a neighbor. Leland's big on being a part of the community. That's why he has that picnic every Memorial Day for the PSBA and that's why he's forced me into…" He let the sentence trail off. "Never mind. You didn't come here to talk about Wagner, McDuffy and Chambers's role in the community and if it had been a normal kind of day, I wouldn't be talking about it either. Have a seat and tell me what I can do for you."

Helplessly, Sarah looked around the office, and finally moved a pile of papers from the chair and sat. "I have a client, well, had a client. I redecorated his offices, an entire floor. It was an extensive job and he still owes me a considerable outstanding balance. Though I've sent him bills, called him on the phone and even sent a certified letter, he hasn't paid me. I'm a small business owner, Donovan. I don't have any assets to fall back on. I pretty much live from hand to mouth. I counted on that money, and things are getting tight.''

That was a huge understatement. Things weren't just tight, they were desperate. She took a deep breath and continued.

"Anyway, I was wondering if you could draw up some paper, or sue him, or whatever it is you do when someone owes you money. And I'm hoping you can do it as soon as possible because I'm really hurting financially.''

"You have a signed contract?" Donovan asked.

She bristled a little at the question and the tone he asked it in. What did he think she was? Totally inept?

"Yes," she answered.

"Did you bring it?" he asked, fingers steepled under his chin as he simply waited for her response.

Okay, maybe she was slightly inept. She should have thought to bring the contract and copies of the letters she'd sent. "I'm sorry. I didn't think to bring it, but I can go get it for you.''

"That's not necessary. Send it over tomorrow.''

"Donovan, I don't know how this works. Do you need a retainer for something like this? If so, I..." It galled Sarah to admit it, but she did, "I don't have it. I'm down to my last nickel, almost literally. When I bought the building, it took most of my savings, and the start-up costs took the rest. I'm broke. I'll pay you as soon as you settle. I'll do whatever it takes.''

Donovan stared at his neighbor as she rattled on and on about money.

Sarah Madison was an attractive woman. She was tall. She was only a couple inches shorter than his six feet. And she had red hair. Her brows were about the same shade. He was pretty sure that meant her hair color was natural, not that it mattered. She had freckles, too. There was just a light sprinkling across her nose. And her eyes. Well, there was something about her grayish blue eyes that—

He cut off the thought.

The color of her eyes didn't matter. Not for what he had in mind.

He'd been sitting in his office all day brooding about where he was going to find a fiancée. And then Sarah Madison had called him personally for an appointment, and he'd known his fiancée was at hand.

He knew her in a casual way. He nodded when he saw her on the square. And there was that one day...

It had been raining. No, not raining, pouring.

One minute the skies had simply opened up and dumped. Donovan had run into the first door—By Design. The sign had just gone up and as he let himself into the room, the bell on the door and the boxes littering the floor were the only indications that someone might actually be using the space.

She'd popped up from behind a box, her hair tucked into a baseball cap, her nose smudged with dirt and had grinned as she said, "We're not quite open for business, as you can see."

She stood and extended a hand. "I'm Sarah. Sarah Madison."

"Donovan," he'd said, giving her hand a perfunctory shake. "I got caught in the downpour."

"Rain like that can't last long. Make yourself at home until it slows down." She'd nodded at a box, still smiling, as if she hadn't noticed he'd given her hand the most cursory shake.

Something about her made him uneasy.

Not in an uneasy, run-for-your-life sort of way. But in a deeper, there-was-something-about-this-woman-he-couldn't-quite-put-his-finger-on, sort of way. And he didn't like things, especially feelings, that he couldn't understand.

Donovan made an immediate decision—he didn't want to understand this woman. So rather than take her up on her offer, he took the coward's way out and said, "It already looks like it's slowing down. I'll just be going."

"If it's slowed at all it's gone from monsoon to simple downpour. Why don't you wait a few more minutes?"

Donovan shook his head. "Thanks, but I have to be going."

He'd run then from her building to his and soaked

himself in the process. Months later he still wasn't sure why.

But she seemed easygoing...malleable. And she needed something from him and that gave him leverage, and that leverage made her perfect.

Fate couldn't have been any kinder when she'd announced she needed his legal expertise and didn't have the money for a retainer.

"Well, Sarah, we're neighbors, and neighbors help each other out."

"Donovan, I know we're not best buddies, but I had hoped you'd feel that way. And I'll sign whatever you want, promising to pay you as soon as that dog Ratgaz pays me."

He drummed his fingers on the desk a moment, and finally said, "Well, maybe there's something else you could do for me. You see, I have a little problem that is right up your alley."

"A decorating problem?"

He could see the relief on her face. She had an expressive face, one that he bet was used to wearing her every emotion. Would she be able to pull a fake engagement off?

Sarah continued, "To be honest, I'd noticed when I walked in what a mess this room is. How on earth do you ever manage to see clients in here?"

"I see them in the meeting room, but that's not—"

"That's not the issue. The issue is, how can you

work in this…well, clutter, Donovan? I'm sure your mother used to tell you a messy room makes for a messy mind. Mine did. Mom liked order. Not a cold institutional order, but a comfortable one. I inherited that from her, that need to make things comfortable, yet orderly. She didn't have a formal business, but Mom decorated a lot of friends' places. And I'll do a great job on yours. I can take this room and do so much with it. Make it serviceable, and yet attractive. And that way if you wanted to see clients here rather than in the meeting room you could do it without blushing with embarrassment."

"I don't blush. Like I said no one usually sees my office, but since you're a neighbor, I thought it might be better to meet in here."

"I'm glad you recognize we're neighbors, Donovan, though to be honest, we've never had a real conversation before today. There was that one day right after I bought the place, but you ran out, despite the fact it was still pouring. You must have had an important meeting. But that initial meeting must have been enough for you to recognize our neighborliness. But people say I'm easy to know, so that must be it, because they don't say you're easy to know. No, they say you're—"

She clapped a hand over her mouth, obviously embarrassed.

"I know what people say about me, and that's fine

with me.'' At least it had always felt fine until this minute as he watched Sarah hem and haw over it.

Time to get things back on track. ''Listen, this favor isn't about my office.''

Her embarrassment forgotten, she grinned. ''The reception area then? Oh, that's almost as good. I mean, this is such an old stately office, and yet the front desk looks like it came from some garage sale, or even worse, from a cardboard box—you know the kind with instructions and even the tools included? It doesn't fit with the ambiance of the building at all, and since it's the first thing clients see when they come in, you want it to make a statement. Something old, that will say to them, we're established, and solid. Something—''

''Sarah.''

She stopped midsentence and took a breath. ''Sorry, sometimes I get carried away. So, why don't you tell me what you want me to decorate?''

''My arm.''

Donovan watched as Sarah tried to digest his cryptic statement. He should have been clearer, but he was nervous.

Oh, he doubted she'd notice, and he certainly would never admit it to anyone, not even to Sarah, but there it was. After all, it wasn't every day he asked a woman to be his fiancée, even if it was just for a night.

He actually thought his palms were sweating, so he placed them on his slacks and covertly wiped them off.

"Pardon?" Sarah finally said.

He folded his now drier hands in front of him on his desk and leaned forward. "Okay, I'm going to lay it on the line, but first I need you to promise that what I say won't go any farther than this office even if you decide not to help me."

She actually crossed her heart. "I promise."

If Donovan was the type, he'd think the gesture was endearing. But he wasn't the type, so he simply said, "Thanks."

"You're welcome." She smiled a tentative smile, and sat back and simply waited for him to start.

He tried to think of the most logical way to present his case. He just needed to treat it as if he was in court making his summation to the jury.

"I want to be a partner in this firm. I deserve to be. I bring in more accounts, more money than any of the other associates. And in another firm, there'd be no problem. I'd be partner by now."

"How is this firm different than other firms?"

"Leland Wagner, that's how. He's living in the last century and doesn't believe a man can be complete and happy unless he has a family. Balance. That's what he calls it."

"And you don't want a family?"

"I don't have time for a family. My job comes first,

which is why I'm the biggest money-machine the firm has."

"If work comes first, then why would you choose to work in a firm that promotes family?"

"I—" Donovan stopped short. She'd stumped him with the question.

He'd never really been sure why he'd chosen to work at Wagner, McDuffy and Chambers. He'd had other offers, better offers in terms of prestige. Yet, something about this firm felt right. It...

"Listen," he said, "that doesn't matter. What matters is Leland thinks I need balance."

"I still don't see where I come in," Sarah said.

"We, Leland and I, were having a meeting, talking about partnership, and he was agreeing I had everything I needed to be a partner...everything but a wife. And that's where you come in."

"I know I must appear dense, but I still don't see where you're going with this," Sarah said.

"Sarah, I know we don't know each other very well. Actually we don't know each other at all, but that doesn't really matter. Leland insists I need a wife to become partner, and I want this position, so I want you to be my—"

Her face lost its color and she asked in a shaky voice, "You want me to be your wife?"

"Not wife," he assured her. Donovan was happy with his life as it was and didn't plan to marry for a long time, if ever. Right now he just wanted to concentrate on furthering his career, and in order to do that he need a... "Fiancée."

"Fiancée?" she repeated, making the word more of a question than a statement.

"Fiancée. And just for one night. Leland and his wife are having a huge blowout anniversary party next week and I told him I'd bring my fiancée. The only problem is, I don't have a fiancée."

"So you lied."

Donovan didn't like the way she made it sound. "I embellished."

"Lied," she insisted. "I'm not your fiancée, but you want me to pose as one. That's a lie."

"You are if you say you are. I mean, we could be engaged, for just one night, and then I'm not lying. We'll simply dissolve our engagement afterward."

"What did you do? Look at your appointment book and say to yourself, *the next single woman who walks in the door I'll ask to be my fiancée?*"

Sarah looked annoyed. More than annoyed, she looked insulted.

And the way she put it, the proposal sounded insulting. Donovan said, "I—"

"Why would you think I'd agree to this? I came here for legal counsel, that's all."

"But this would help you," he insisted.

"How could my playing your fiancée for a night help me?" she asked. There was a furrow on her brow, as her face got all tight with annoyance.

For the first time in a long time, Donovan wasn't quite sure what to say to make this better. In the courtroom he was never at a loss. He prepared his case, knew it inside out and was so prepared that nothing could throw him off his rhythm. But he hadn't had enough time to prepare for this. Actually all the time in the world couldn't have prepared him for this.

Mentally he tried to put some tactical offense together.

"You said you were in financial straits."

"I won't be after this deadbeat pays me. Things will go back to being merely tight. But I knew things would be tight when I bought the store. I was willing to scrimp for a few years in order to own something...something that's all mine. By Design has so much potential. All I need is to get it off the ground. If you can get Ratgaz to pay, I'll be okay."

"And I will. But you shouldn't be so dependent on one job. Plus, sometimes the courts move slowly. And even if we reach a settlement, it could be a while. What if in the meantime you had other jobs? Jobs that would pay the bills while you waited?"

"Pretending to be your fiancée would get me other jobs?" Sarah asked.

"Leland Wagner is a very well respected man within the community. Anyone who's anyone in Erie will be at this party. And I'll promise to introduce you around."

"Really, Mr. Donovan—"

"When did I become Mr. Donovan?" He was surprised by how much he didn't like the cold distance in her tone.

"The minute you asked me to play a role in your absurd charade." She rose and started to the door. "Thank you for seeing me."

"Sarah, what about your case?" Donovan asked.

"I'll handle it. I'll handle everything," she said as she walked out of his office.

Chapter Two

"I'll handle it. You'll have the money soon," Sarah promised yet another creditor and hung up the phone.

This one was threatening to turn off her electricity if she didn't make a payment, pronto.

She'd spent the night thinking about Donovan's odd offer. Fiancée for a night?

Who would it hurt? People got engaged and then, for one reason or another, broke things off all the time. That's all they'd do. They'd be engaged, but they'd know that there was a specific length to their engagement, that it would never lead to marriage.

And if she got a few jobs out of it, well that would be all the better. It wouldn't be hurting anyone because she was good, very good at what she did. Anyone who signed on with her got their money's worth and then some. Just a few high profile jobs, and word of mouth would take care of her money worries.

Plus, Donovan would get the Rat to pay what he owed. This short-term engagement would mean the end of Sarah's money worries.

And Donovan? He'd get his partnership.

He was right, holding the partnership hostage until he married wasn't the way business should be done. Advances, jobs, partnerships should be awarded based on merit not on any sort of status, marriage or otherwise.

So actually, if she did this she'd be balancing the scales of justice. Donovan's boss had put an unfair condition on his advancement and she'd just be getting rid of that unfair obstacle.

Sarah Jane Madison, defender of workers' rights.

Even as she thought the words, even as much as she'd like to believe she was that altruistic, the truth was, she needed Donovan's help, and she needed any jobs he could steer her way.

She wasn't going to lie to herself about her motives, but she would be more comfortable knowing they weren't hurting anyone and wouldn't be lying. They just wouldn't disclose the full nature of their relationship.

She thought about calling Donovan, but decided against it. She needed to do this in person. She left the shop, locked the door and walked next door to Wagner, McDuffy and Chambers.

"You're back," Amelia said by way of a greeting. "I didn't expect to see you so soon."

"I need to see Donovan."

"Do you have another appointment?" Amelia asked, even as she started thumbing through her appointment calendar.

"No," Sarah admitted. "But he'll see me, unless he's with a client."

"He doesn't have any clients coming in this afternoon, but Donovan is generally a stickler about things like appointments. He's working on some huge contract, and he hates to be interrupted." Amelia looked worried.

"He'll see me," Sarah assured her. "And he won't be mad. I promise."

Looking doubtful, Amelia punched three buttons on her phone. "Mr. Donovan, Sarah Madison from next door is here to see you again. She doesn't have an appointment, but it sounds… Okay, I will."

Amelia hung up the phone and silently studied Sarah. "Just what's going on between the two of you?"

"What do you mean?" Sarah asked.

"I mean, not only did Donovan say send you right up, but he almost sounded pleased. The Iceman doesn't show emotion, especially not pleasure. So what did you do to him last night?"

"Who said it was last night and not some other

night?'' Sarah refused to lie to Amelia, but a little misdirection might be in order.

Sarah chatted with Amelia but they weren't bosom buddies—though Sarah hoped their friendship continued. However, Amelia might think it was funny if she found out that Donovan and Sarah were engaged. But if she thought that they'd been dating on the sly...

''What do you mean by that?'' Amelia asked, her eyes narrowing, almost as if she could kick in an X-ray vision and see whatever secrets Sarah was keeping from her.

''Nothing. I shouldn't have said that. As you said, Donovan can be a stickler about some things. He's a private man.'' She started up the stairs.

''Wait a minute,'' Amelia called after her. ''You can't just leave me hanging.''

''Like I said, Donovan's a private man and I respect that. I hope you do as well. I'd prefer you didn't mention these little appointments to anyone.''

''You sly dog.'' Admiration tinged Amelia's voice. ''You're dating him. How long?''

''Amelia, I really can't talk about it.''

''I won't tell a soul,'' she promised.

''Thanks. But after all, what could you tell them? I have a business appointment. That's all. And I better get going. Donovan hates to be kept waiting.'' She started up the stairs again. ''Don't worry, I know the way up.'' Sarah left before Amelia could ask her anything else.

She walked up the stairs slowly, trying to steady her racing heart. After all, it was only for one night.

Only for one night.

Only for one night.

She chanted the phrase as she climbed each step. Like Cinderella, she'd have her one ball, and then return to her real life.

She was outside Donovan's door all too soon. She knocked.

"Come in."

She opened the door and was struck again by the clutter. She purposely ignored it and concentrated on the task at hand.

"Sarah?" Donovan said, rising. "I didn't expect to see you back here. After yesterday, I figured you'd never want to talk to me again. I realize that it's a crazy idea—"

"Sit down, Donovan."

He did, and she took the same chair she'd sat in the day before. Yesterday she'd sat here totally disconcerted by Donovan's suggestion. And today she was ready to go along with it. What a difference twenty-four hours could make.

"Sarah, I—"

She cut him off, afraid if she didn't get it out now, she never would. "Just say the words."

"Pardon?" His brow furrowed, as if he was trying to understand something.

What was there to understand? Sarah had thought

the sentence was clear enough, but obviously not for a man. So she laid it on the line. "Ask me to marry you."

Before he could speak, she stopped him. "No, better yet, invite me to a romantic dinner tonight, and pop the question. Then I'm not lying to your friends, or to anyone. We might as well get that straight right here and now. I won't lie, and I will be your fiancée for the party. But when they ask me about how you proposed, I won't lie. I'd rather not say you asked me in your messy office, so think of something romantic and ask me tonight at dinner."

"A romantic proposal?" Donovan asked slowly, as if she'd totally shocked him.

Sarah didn't feel any pity. After all, asking for a romantic proposal wasn't nearly as shocking as asking for a temporary fiancée.

"I wouldn't know where to start," he said.

"Well, figure it out." She stood. She needed to get out of here. "You can pick me up at the store at six." She started for the door.

Donovan stopped her by asking, "What changed your mind?"

Sarah turned around and faced him again. "You're right, I need your help and this charade won't hurt anyone. Plus, we really won't be lying. This will just be the shortest engagement in history."

"I still don't understand why I have to be romantic. Who will know?" he asked.

"I will. And I'll be able to tell anyone who asks how romantic you were. Let's face it, The Iceman image could use a little warming up. This will help. I mean, being in control in the courtroom is one thing, but being so in control the rest of the time is not a positive image to put forth."

"I like being The Iceman."

"You would. But I don't want to be engaged to a Sno-Kone, so I want a romantic proposal. Like I said, you can pick me up at six."

Before he could protest, she walked out of the room and shut the door behind her. She leaned against it and let out a huge breath she hadn't realized she'd been holding.

She'd done it. She'd—

The door pulled open and Sarah, still leaning against, fell inward with the loss of support.

Donovan caught her in his arms. And for a moment it almost felt like an embrace more than a simple catch. He might be called The Iceman, but Donovan's arms felt warm and inviting.

Warm and inviting? What was she thinking?

"Thanks," she said, and hurriedly moved away from him. "Did you want something else?"

"Your ring size," he said.

Sarah unconsciously touched her ring finger. "Ring size?"

"You'll need an engagement ring. I mean if you're worried about everyone knowing that I'm not the icy man they think, I'll need to impress them with a nice ring. I'll just make sure the jeweler will let me return it.''

"Well, as long as you can return it, it's probably a good idea. Seven and a half should do it, I think.''

"Seven and a half," he repeated. "Fine. I'll see you at six." He went back in his office and shut the door. As if on autopilot, Sarah walked down the stairs.

She'd done it, she thought as she reached the foyer in a daze. Even when Amelia said her name she just gave a faint wave and left, walked out of the building, down the stairs and toward her office.

She'd done it, she thought again as she let herself into her office and sank into one of the plush chairs that she'd dreamed would be filled with clients.

She'd done it. Sarah put her head down in her hands and groaned.

She'd done it.

The problem was, she wasn't sure just what she'd done.

Donovan felt like a schoolboy as he patted his pocket for the umpteenth time to reassure himself the ring was still there. It was.

He gave himself a mental shake. There was no reason he should be nervous. It wasn't as if this were a real marriage proposal. He hardly knew Sarah Madison. She was simply convenient. She needed him, and he needed her.

There had been a time when marriages had been arranged for less of a reason than he had—than *they* had. Not that this was ever going to be a marriage.

She was just his fake fiancée, and only for one night.

Well, the party wasn't until next weekend, so more than one night, actually. But as soon as the party was over, the engagement would be, too. And that's why he shouldn't be nervous, he told himself.

But telling and feeling were two separate things, he discovered, because he was still nervous.

"Are you okay, Mr. Donovan?" Amelia asked.

"I'm fine," he said. But he wondered if that was true. He was about to get engaged to a woman he didn't even know.

"You don't look fine, if you don't mind me saying so," Amelia said.

"And if I do mind you saying so?" he snapped.

He wished he could take the words back when he saw her face fall. Amelia was just being kind. He had no right to take his anxiety out on her.

"Sorry," he said. "You're right, I'm not quite myself. I've got a splitting headache."

"Oh, well don't go until you've taken something." She rummaged in her desk drawer.

Sarah was right, he thought. The desk didn't fit the rest of the room. They needed something older, something more in keeping with the air of elegance the one hundred and fifty year old former home exuded.

Maybe he could talk Leland into hiring Sarah to redecorate?

No. What was he thinking? Once this engagement was over, if he truly had lost a fiancée, he wouldn't want Sarah hanging around too much. Her working here wouldn't be wise.

"Here," said Amelia, handing him two white pills. "Let me get you a glass of water."

She was gone before he could tell her not to bother, and was back a moment later with a paper cup from the watercooler.

"Thanks, Amelia."

She smiled shyly. "No problem, Mr. Donovan."

Dutifully he took the two pills, draining the glass. He tossed it in the garbage can and asked, "Amelia, how long have you worked here?"

"Two and a half years, sir." She looked nervous again.

Iceman. That's what people called him behind his back. Did he intimidate Amelia? He'd never really thought about it before, but now that he did, the thought didn't sit right.

Wanting to put her at ease, he said, "And for that entire time I've called you Amelia, and you've referred to me as Mr. Donovan. Don't you think it's time that changed?"

"Changed, sir?" she asked, her voice little more than a squeak.

"Donovan, Amelia. Just call me Donovan. At least when there aren't any clients hanging around."

Nervousness vanished and her smile blossomed. "Thank you, sir."

"Thanks for the help, and for the aspirin," he said.

"Anytime…Donovan."

Knowing he was stalling and couldn't drag out this conversation with Amelia any longer, he left the office and walked the too-few-steps next door to Sarah's. He opened the door and the little bell over it chimed a merry high-pitched clanging.

He stepped inside and realized that he'd never ventured into Sarah's shop since that rainy day. She'd been unpacking boxes then.

Now? He stood just inside the door and studied the room, as if he could get a glimpse of who this woman he was about to be engaged to really was.

The room was done in blue. Every shade of blue imaginable, with bits of yellow and red scattered throughout. High, overstuffed chairs, small end tables, and lamps, rather than any overhead lighting. Donovan was no decorator, but he liked the effect. It was a warm and inviting space. Rather like Sarah herself.

Now where did that come from? *Warm and inviting?* No, Sarah was desperate. That's the only reason she'd agreed to his plan.

Well, he'd keep his end of the bargain as long as

she kept hers. He'd get her the money she was owed, and maybe even be the catalyst for a few new decorating opportunities.

"Donovan," she said.

He hadn't heard her come into the room and started at the sound of her voice. He couldn't help but notice that she looked great. She had on a red dress that was made of some light, airy material. It swished as she walked. He liked the way it caressed her body. With any other woman, it would make him want to caress her as well. But not Sarah. This was just business, he reminded himself.

He suddenly felt awkward and didn't like it, so he pushed the feeling away, and said, "Are you ready?"

She nodded.

"My car's across the park."

They walked in silence, side by side, across the street and through one of the tree-lined twin blocks that made up the park at the center of Perry Square. A fat squirrel sat in the middle of the sidewalk, apparently not the least bit intimidated by them as they walked toward the police station.

"I love the park," Sarah said. "I like to sit here by the gazebo and eat."

"I know." Donovan could have kicked himself as he heard the words come out of his mouth.

"You know?"

"Well, my office looks out over the park, and

sometimes I can see you out here eating. You like to feed the squirrels your leftovers.''

''You've watched me?'' she asked.

''Not really watched, just noticed you from time to time.''

Since that day in the rain, it seemed he couldn't escape noticing Sarah. He prided himself in only offering the merest nod if their paths actually crossed. But he could see her comings and goings through the park, simply because he had a perfect vantage from his office's front window.

''Oh,'' she said.

She looked uncomfortable. But she couldn't be as uncomfortable as Donovan felt. ''It's not as if I'm spying on you, or anything. It's just that I'm on the second story and my office looks down on the park and—''

''It's okay, Donovan. I believe you. After all, why would you spy on someone like me?''

''What do you mean, someone like you?''

She shrugged. ''I mean, I've seen you leave your office with women on occasion....''

Donovan wondered if she'd noticed him as well. She'd seen him leave his office with women? She must have. The thought brightened his mood a bit. He realized she was still talking and focused on what she was saying.

''...and I know I'm not your type. I've got this awful hair, and freckles. I've always thought I looked more like someone's kid sister than a woman in my own right.''

''You're a beautiful lady, Sarah.'' Though he knew it was him, it felt as if someone else had just said those words.

He tried to think of something else to say. But thinking and talking around Sarah didn't seem to be in the cards.

More words came tumbling out of his mouth, seemingly by their own volition. ''If you're not my type it's only because you're the kind of woman who makes a man think of settling down. Not that I'm thinking about settling down. I have a practice to build, and that doesn't leave time for anything else. If I ever marry, I'd want to be able to devote myself to the relationship, not begrudge it the time it takes. The women I date understand that it's casual. You're just not the casual type.''

There. He might have gotten off to a rocky start, but he felt he'd finished well.

''Not the casual type,'' Sarah repeated. ''Which is why I'm perfect for this ruse.''

''Oh, but it's not a ruse, is it? We will be officially engaged. You won't be lying.''

They reached his car and Donovan held the door open for her. It was a short drive down State Street, one that they made in silence. As they reached the last hill before the bayfront, Donovan stared at Erie's dock. It was crowded with cars, full of people and activity.

Donovan loved the bay. He remembered coming down here with friends when he was a boy. It hadn't been this clean and touristy then. It had been a working bay area. Industry, fishing boats.

The last ten years or so the waterfront had shifted from industry to tourism. New restaurants, a new dock renamed Dobbins Landing. A permanent home for, and museum built around, the *Brig Niagra*, the reconstructed ship from the Battle of Lake Erie. A new library.

He loved it down here.

Donovan realized Sarah was silent on her side of the car.

"I thought we'd take the dinner cruise," he said more to break the silence than anything else. "I've done some work for the line, and they squeezed us in. Is giving you a ring on the top deck of a boat right at sunset romantic enough?"

"Yes," was her monosyllabic response.

"Good." He slipped the car into a parking space and looked at Sarah. She looked nervous, rather like Amelia had earlier.

The Iceman.

Did he intimidate her? For some reason the thought of Sarah being ill at ease with him didn't sit well.

"Let's go," he said, trying to sound soothing. "They're already boarding."

* * *

Sarah had pushed around her dinner more than eaten it. And though Donovan had tried to start a number of conversations, they'd all fallen flat, and it was her fault. She was unbelievably nervous, and that didn't make any sense. This wasn't for real.

But she was thankful dinner was over. The dinner cruise would be over soon and she'd go home, an engaged woman. One small party next week, and she'd be unengaged.

She glanced at the man standing next to her on the top deck of the paddle boat. He was certainly good looking. Taller than her, which was nice for a change. At five ten, she frequently dwarfed the men she dated.

Donovan had silky looking black hair with this one little piece that wouldn't quite stay in the neat style he wore. That one piece seemed to call to her. She'd like to smooth it into place, but she wouldn't dare. It would be too familiar. Too intimate.

Yes, he was good-looking, and successful and… well, maybe a small piece of Sarah wondered what it would be like if this was all for real.

No. She shouldn't imagine it. Donovan was The Iceman and this was business, pure and simple.

"I don't think I could have timed this better," he said, startling her.

"Better?" she asked.

"The sun is setting and we're out in the middle of the bay. So…"

He reached into his pants pocked and took out a small, black velvet box. "Sarah, would you do me the honor of being my fiancée?"

He opened the lid. "I know it won't be for long, and I know that it won't be quite what a normal engagement is, but I promise that I'll take care of your legal problems and I'll see to it that you meet people that can help your business."

He took a ring from the box. It was a small gold band, a claddagh. There was a small, well-polished stone with a greenish tinge to it, shaped like a heart in the center. It wasn't a gemstone, it looked like marble.

Donovan slid it on her finger.

Sarah jumped. Donovan's touching her was disconcerting.

"I didn't even have to get it sized," he said.

As soon as the ring was on her finger, she pulled her hand back and tried to act as if she'd done it in order to study the ring, and not because his touch bothered her.

"My answer is, yes, I'll be your fiancée until after the party." She studied the ring. "Where did you get this?"

If she didn't know better, Sarah would think Donovan was blushing. But that reddish tinge in his cheeks must have simply been a reflection of the rosy glow of the sunset.

"It was my grandmother's, but it's older than her.

Family legend has it that when Patrick O'Donovan emigrated to the U.S. with his young wife Brigit, he promised he'd bring her back to Ireland someday and gave her this ring to seal the promise. The stone? It's Connemarra marble. He gave her a piece of Ireland's heart as well as his own.''

''And did they?'' Sarah twirled the ring on her finger, admiring it even more now.

''No. She died before they could go back and he didn't have the heart to go without her. It's come through the family since then. My grandfather gave it to my grandmother who wore it every day. It's come down the generations with a promise that a Donovan would take the woman he loved back to Ireland.

''My grandparents were planning the trip, but my grandfather passed away before they had a chance to go. My grandmother couldn't go without him, either. The ring should have passed to my mother, but she never liked it—it's not her style—so it came to me. My grandmother made me promise that someday I'd go back to Ireland with the woman I loved. She told me not to wait, like they had. Love was precious and life was precarious. She told me to savor both.''

''Donovan. That's a beautiful family story. But I can't wear this.'' Sarah tugged at the ring, but it didn't slide off with the ease it had slid on.

His hand covered hers, stopping her from trying to pull it off. ''Why not?''

"It's special. It's not just some pawn-store ring that would suffice for a less-than-real engagement. This—" she flashed the ring "—should go on the finger of the woman you someday truly love and plan to marry. Not just on a fake fiancée."

"You wanted special, you've got it. That ring, this proposal is as special as I can get. Wear it."

"But—"

"Please?"

Sarah touched the small stone. It still didn't seem right to wear a family heirloom—more than that, a family legend—but she found herself unable to say no to Donovan.

"All right," she heard herself agreeing.

She needed to get her head out of the clouds and back to the matter at hand. "I should tell you that I was thinking about our engagement and realized you hadn't taken into account one simple problem—Amelia.

"We're not friends, exactly. I've been so busy with the store, that I don't really have time to socialize. But we're friendly, and I think that we will be friends. We've met a few times for lunch. We've chatted about this and that, but I've never mentioned dating you. I'm afraid she'll find it suspicious that we're all of a sudden engaged. So earlier, when I came to the office, I sort of insinuated that there might be something between us, something that had nothing to do with business. I let her think we'd been dating for a while on the sly. I hope that will be enough to make her swallow this story. After all, you're known for being a private person, and I'll just explain you felt what went on between us was private and didn't want it gossiped about at the firm.''

"That should work. Maybe you should call now and again. Let her get used to the idea,'' he said.

Sarah nodded. That made sense. ''Maybe we should slip away to the park for lunch, where anyone at the firm who glances out the window could see us.''

"Okay.''

It was as if they'd used up all the words they had to say. And maybe they had. It wasn't as if they were even friends, Sarah thought. They stood silently at the railing of the upper deck as the paddle boat began to maneuver back beside the dock.

Finally the engines stopped and Sarah looked down over the railing and saw the crew lowering the gangplank.

"I guess it's time to go,'' Sarah said, breaking their long silence.

"How about a quick lunch on Wednesday. And then I'll see you when I pick you up for the party next Saturday. It's a dinner thing, so I'll come by about five? Leland said they're eating about six-thirty.''

"Five is fine.'' They walked down the stairs to the dinner level of the ship, then through the dining room to the gangplank. Donovan took her arm as they crossed the street to his car.

"Where to?"

"Uh, my car's at the store, so you can drop me there." Sarah didn't want to admit that in order to conserve desperately needed money, she was using her office as a home.

The large armoire in the back didn't hold business items, but her wardrobe. The rest of her personal belongings were stacked in boxes in the storeroom.

If she could get the Rat to pay his debt, and maybe land a few more jobs, she could start looking for a small place. Until then, her office was fine, but it wasn't something Donovan needed to know. After all, it had no bearing on this…whatever this was between them. And soon she'd have an apartment.

It was easier to dream about her future apartment than to dwell on the silence that enveloped the car as they rode back up State Street to Perry Square.

"So, I'll see you Wednesday about eleven," Donovan said.

Sarah nodded. "I'll be ready. About the party, I assume it's dressy?"

"I guess. I'm wearing a suit." She closed the door and he lowered the electric window. "Oh, and fax that contract over to the office tomorrow, along with any other information you have about that client. I'll get started on it. Maybe I can tell you something by Wednesday."

"Okay, I will," she promised and started walking toward the store.

"And Sarah?" he called.

She turned around. "Yes?"

"Thank you." He rolled up the window and drove away.

He was probably going home. Sarah realized she didn't even know where he lived. They'd have to have a crash course on each others lives before they got to the party.

How were they ever going to pull this off? Somehow Sarah had to make a party full of strangers believe that she'd cracked The Iceman's hard shell and reached the man inside. She just wasn't sure if she could do it.

Chapter Three

Their get-together on Wednesday had been a bust. Donovan had had some emergency and canceled.

Sarah hadn't complained. Actually she'd been secretly relieved. She was reluctant to spend more time with him than necessary and had considered finding some excuse to cancel herself. But missing Wednesday's lunch meant that they hadn't had any time to prepare for tonight.

The drive to the party was a crash course in their respective histories.

"My mother's name is Eda," Donovan said.

"Eda," Sarah repeated dutifully.

She felt as if she was cramming for a test as she tried to squeeze as much Donovan information as she could into the short drive to the party.

"Eda," he said again. "Her folks were second generation German immigrants. My father's name is Mike. Anyway, Mom and Dad live in Orlando now. No brothers. No sisters. Some aunts, uncles and cousins, but none I'm close to. My grandmother lived with us after my grandfather died. She watched me a lot because they both worked. Not just worked, *had careers.*"

Sarah thought she heard a lance of pain in that statement, but Donovan kept speaking, and she didn't have time to really analyze it.

"I grew up in Erie," he continued. "Went to Prep, then to Mercyhurst College, and finally to law school in Pittsburgh. Wagner, McDuffy and Chambers hired me right out of school. No significant relationships. Oh, and I live in the Bayfront Condos."

"Can I ask a question? Why Wagner, McDuffy and Chambers? I mean, given your reputation..." She paused.

"As The Iceman. You can say it."

"It's just that, it seems out of character to choose such a family oriented firm. A place that insists you're married before you can be a partner."

Donovan was silent. She'd asked the question before and hadn't gotten an answer. His silence indicated she probably wasn't getting one this time, either. She couldn't tell if he was angry or thinking, but either way, she realized it wasn't any of her business where Donovan chose to work. That didn't stop her from wondering about his choice.

"I'm sorry," she finally said when the silence weighed too heavily on her. "I didn't mean to overstep myself. You don't have to answer. It doesn't have any bearing on us. Let's just finish this."

Sarah started rattling off facts, "My dad's name is Kevin. My mom's name is Jane. I'm named after her. Sarah Jane. Hey, that reminds me, what's your full name?"

They were driving down Lakeshore Drive, one of the most beautiful sections of Erie, in Sarah's opinion. The streets were tree-lined, and the homes with palatial elegance overlooked the bay. She sighed as she watched out her window. It was easier to concentrate on the street's beauty than worry about what she and Donovan were about to try to pull off.

"My full name?" he asked. "You'd never be permitted to use it, so it's not an issue."

"But I should know it," she pressed, more because it seemed to make him uncomfortable, than because she thought she needed to know the information. She doubted it would come up in conversation.

"It can't be that bad," she added. "And I'll probably keep pestering you until you tell me, so you might as well tell me now and save yourself all the hassles. Why I could go on, and on, and on—"

He cut her off. "It's Elias. Elias Augustus Donovan."

"Wow," she said, trying to suppress a giggle. "Elias Augustus Donovan. That's a mouthful."

"You're not laughing at my name, are you?" he asked, a dangerous tone in his voice.

"Elias Augustus? No, no of course I'm not." The small giggle that escaped may have given her away.

Yep. It had.

Donovan turned and glared at her, and rather than being intimidated, Sarah laughed harder.

"Elias," she started, using his first name for the first time.

The only description for his response was a growl.

"Donovan," she corrected herself, holding back more laughter, but unable to keep from smiling. "I meant to say Donovan, though I like Elias. You sound, I don't know, more approachable as an Elias."

"I don't want to be approachable, so it's Donovan. Now, finish up on your family stuff. We're almost there."

"Like I said, my dad's name is Kevin. He just retired last year, and my parents are on a six-month biking tour of Europe."

"Biking?" he asked.

"They're health nuts—what can I say? What else? We're from Meadeville, but Dad's company transferred him my freshman year of college to Erie. I worked for a decorator in Pittsburgh right out of school. My aunt left me a small trust that I gained access to when I was twenty-five, and I'd saved everything I could while working. I knew I wanted to work for myself. So when the opportunity presented itself I took it. I moved here to be close to Mom and Dad, but Dad took an early retirement and they've been traveling since. Starting By Design took all the money I had, which is why I'm in such dire straits now.''

''Couldn't your parents help you out?''

''They could, but I wouldn't ask. By Design is mine. I want to do it on my own.''

Thank heaven her parents had sold the house when her father retired. They planned to buy something smaller when they returned from Europe. By then, Sarah would have her own place and they'd never know she was living out of her office.

She didn't even want to think of their reaction. They'd be livid, thinking of her reduced state. They'd insist on helping her out, and they wouldn't understand that Sarah wanted and needed to do this on her own.

And of course, if they found out about her fake engagement...

Sarah was saved from thoughts of her parents' ire as Donovan pulled into a driveway and parked behind a line of cars.

Before he got out of the car, Donovan said, ''We're here, but there's one big question left, how did we start dating?''

Sarah got out of the car as well and said, ''You

watched me in the park—that much is true. I caught your eye. Okay, so maybe we're embellishing that a bit, but you asked me out to dinner, and next thing I knew, you found you couldn't live without me and were proposing. That's true, too, only our dinner was right before the proposal.''

"I'm not going to comment on the *couldn't live without you* part. It's good enough.'' He led her up the stone walkway to the front door of the huge, brick colonial home.

"Favorite color?'' she asked in a hushed tone as he knocked on the door.

"Black.''

"Black? That's not a color. It can't be your favorite.'' Who liked black the best? She looked at the man next to her. He was dressed in a well-tailored black suit that added to his dark hair and complexion, giving him a dangerous look.

Yeah, that his favorite color was black made sense. It suited his look and his mood.

"What's yours?'' he asked.

"Yellow.'' Her dress tonight was more gold than yellow, but she thought it looked sunny, yet elegant, and wondered if Donovan had even noticed that she'd bought something new to impress his friends—a dress she couldn't afford.

Probably not.

"Yellow?'' He snorted. "Figures.''

The front door opened and a silver-haired man

stepped out to greet them. "Donovan. So it's true. You finally found someone who could put up with you." He extended his hand. "Leland, Leland Wagner, Miss...Donovan didn't tell me your name, but you look very familiar."

"I'm Sarah Madison, Mr. Wagner. I bought the small storefront next to the firm a few months ago. By Design? We've met, but only in passing."

"Well, it will be good to actually get a chance to visit with you tonight. Now, come in and let me introduce you around."

Sarah wasn't sure what she expected, but it wasn't Leland Wagner escorting them through his home and out onto the back patio area where a throng of people were milling around. He stood just outside the doorway, his arm looped through Sarah's, sandwiching her between himself and Donovan.

"Can I have your attention everyone?" he practically shouted in order to be heard above the noise.

The talking died almost immediately as all the guests turned and looked expectantly at their host.

"I want to make a very important introduction. Some of you know Sarah Madison whose business, By Design, is located next to the office. But there's something about Sarah you might not be aware of. You see, I'd like to introduce her tonight not as a business neighbor of the firm, but as the future Mrs. Elias Donovan."

And so the charade began, Sarah thought as she waited for the party's reaction.

A pin dropping would have sounded like a bullet, the group's response was so silent.

Sarah glanced at Donovan standing next to her wearing an unreadable expression and then back at the sea of strangers who were staring at them.

Suddenly, as if some dam had burst, the crowd all started clapping and Sarah found herself swallowed by a sea of people congratulating her.

"How'd you do it?" seemed to be the question of the evening.

The first time Sarah had asked, "How did I do what?" but only the first time.

She quickly realized the question truly was, *How did you melt The Iceman?*

She felt embarrassed as she launched into their true, but carefully worded, story.

The women *oohed* over her ring and the story that accompanied that.

"So, is he taking you to Ireland for your honeymoon?" Hanni Ashford, Leland's daughter, asked. Her two sisters, Liesl and Brigitta, nodded their heads, as if she'd already answered an affirmative.

"Uh, we haven't got far enough to plan a honeymoon yet," Sarah answered. There wouldn't be any honeymoon. Heck, there wasn't even going to be a wedding. Not that she was telling the women that.

But she would keep reminding herself of the fact that this was all a sham.

"How about the wedding? What do you have planned for that? Tell us everything," Brigitta demanded.

The three Wagner girls were all various shades of brunette. Hanni's hair had reddish undertones, Liesl's had blondish highlights, and Brigitta's was a rich sable brown. They were all in their late thirties, maybe early forties, and they were all eager to welcome Sarah *into the family*.

"Actually we haven't got as far as planning the wedding, either. This engagement is still rather new and we're adjusting to that before we add the stress of planning a wedding and honeymoon."

Liesl frowned, "You don't have anything planned yet?"

"Not even a time of year you want to marry in?" Hanni asked. "I mean, I always wanted a July wedding. And it's just what I got. Out on the beach at sunset. Come on, Sarah. Every little girl always dreams about her wedding."

"Fall," Sarah said, anxious to give them something, hoping it would be enough to satisfy them. "When the leaves are at the height of their color."

"Fall? Why it's already late August, September next week. It takes months to plan a wedding. How on earth are you going to plan one in just a few weeks?"

Darn. She should have said spring. Or even next summer. Yeah, next summer would have been better. "Well, maybe we'll just wait until next year."

There, that was a perfect solution. Set the wedding date over a year from now. No one would expect her to have any specifics then.

But Sarah had miscalculated. Liesl sighed and said, "Oh, no. You can't make Donovan wait that long. Why anyone can see, just by looking at the two of you, how much in love you are."

Sarah decided at that very moment that she should have forgotten about interior decorating and gone into acting, because it took an Academy Award–winning performance to keep a straight face at that proclamation.

"I'm sure Donovan cares enough to be willing to wait while I plan my dream wedding. Outdoors, autumn colors for my attendants. The trees outshining anything any decorator could come up with…"

"Well, we won't have it," Brigitta said, cutting off Sarah's musings. She looked across the room and waved her hand. "Dad? Could you come here?"

Leland Wagner walked over to the group. "I see you've met my girls," he said with a genuine smile on his face.

Guilt stabbed at Sarah. Leland was a lovely man. So were his *girls,* though she doubted anyone else would dare call the trio girls.

Everyone she'd met was sweet. Warm and welcoming. And here she was lying to all of them. No matter that there was a real, short-term engagement. It didn't do anything to assuage her guilt.

"Dad," Brigitta said. "Sarah's always dreamed of a fall wedding and is planning to wait until next year so she can get it. Anyone with eyes can see that waiting that long will kill her and Donovan. But it's too hard to plan a wedding to expect her to get it all done in just a few months on her own, but—"

Hanni suddenly grinned and continued, "Yeah, but if she isn't doing it on her own…"

Liesl piped up, "And had help and a place to host the wedding, somewhere with trees and a beautiful view."

"Like here," Brigitta said.

"Here? Why what a wonderful idea," Leland said.

"Really, that's so kind of all of you, but Donovan and I wouldn't think of putting you out that way."

"Nonsense," Leland said. "Let me get…oh, there she is. Dorothy."

His wife, a white-haired lady with a smile that hadn't dimmed even once all evening walked over. Her arm snuck around her husband's waist. "Yes, dear?"

"The girls discovered that Sarah here always wanted an autumn wedding. But you know how hard it is to book a place with such short notice. She was going to wait until next year, but they suggested we do it here."

"We'll take care of everything, Mom," Hanni promised.

If it was possible, Dorothy Wagner's smile burned even brighter as she said, "Oh, no you won't. I haven't got to plan a wedding in a long time. Why, Brigitta, it's been years since you and Marty were married."

She stopped short and turned to Sarah. "Of course, we don't want to step on your mother's toes. Maybe I can call her—"

"My parents are biking in Europe. They won't be home until mid-October."

"Oh, that's perfect. She'll be home just in time for the wedding. Oh, this is going to be fun."

Another woman joined the group. "What will be fun?" she asked, then spotted Sarah in the group. "Sarah, I'm sure you've met so many people tonight you'll never keep us all straight. I'm Lori. I'm another lawyer at the firm."

"I've seen you going to and fro," Sarah said.

Amelia came over as well. "Hey, this looks like the group to be in. What's up?"

"Sarah's getting married," Brigitta said.

What had happened to this conversation? Sarah felt as if she'd been swept out to sea without even a life-vest. "And I thank you all for wanting to help with the wedding, but—"

"But nothing," Dorothy said. "It will be our pleasure. So what do you have in mind?"

"She wants an outdoor wedding, Mom," Hanni said.

"When the foliage is at its height of color," Liesl added.

"Of course, we'd need a tent in case it rains," Dorothy mused aloud.

"Or snowed," Brigitta said.

Everyone just stared at her.

"This is Erie after all," she said with a shrug. "Snow in October isn't unheard of, or even particularly unexpected."

At that, the women all laughed, and the planning went on and on. What colors? How many bridesmaids? How big was her family? Donovan's?

Dorothy knew a judge she was sure they could get to officiate.

Sarah kept trying to protest, but before she knew it she was in the thick of Wagners and associates, planning bridesmaids' dresses and talking about invitations.

She scanned the room, praying Donovan would ride to her rescue.

Donovan couldn't help but watch Sarah surrounded by his colleagues and their families. People were flocking to her. Mainly the women of the firm, but there was Leland, in the thick of things.

"You look nervous," Larry Mackenzie, or Mac as

he was usually called, said. "Worried about what they're saying about you, maybe?"

"Saying about me? Why would they be saying anything about me?"

Mac laughed. "Come on, Donovan. You put a group of women that big together, and of course they're saying things about you. About all the men here, probably. I mean, there's Amelia. I'm sure she's talking about all the men here. Probably I'm top of her hit list. She doesn't like me much."

"Why would you think that?"

"Because last week, she said—" he raised his pitch and spoke in a fairly good imitation of Amelia "—'Larry Mackenzie, I don't like you very much.'"

"What did you do?" Donovan asked.

"What did I do? Why would you assume I did anything? I never understood why Leland hired that woman. She's talkative and—"

"Talkative is just another word for gregarious and friendly. That's the kind of qualities you want in a receptionist."

"Oh, there you go. It's happened." Mac sounded utterly dejected.

"What's happened?"

"You got engaged, and she's turned your brain to mush. This can't be the same Donovan who's worked at Wagner, McDuffy and Chambers for the last six years. Why, you're almost soft."

"I'm not. It's just that—"

"Don't explain." Mac tossed up his hands and shook his head. "Not one thing. I don't want to be polluted by your altered mentality. As a matter of fact, don't say another word. My heart can't take too many more surprises tonight. First you—our own personal Lothario and *my* personal hero—turn up engaged, and now you're defending Amelia. I'm going to get a drink. A big one."

"Mac," Donovan called, but the big man was already walking toward the bar.

Donovan stood against the corner and watched the group of women. They were laughing. Sarah, too. Anyone watching them all together would think they'd known each other forever, not just for a few hours. Sarah looked totally at home with the group.

He'd told her he'd seen her eating lunch in the park now and then. What he didn't mention was watching for her had become part of his daily schedule. He'd start peering at the clock about eleven-thirty, just waiting until noon to see if she was going to show up.

Some days she didn't. He assumed those were days she had business luncheons, or other appointments. And he would never admit it to her—he barely admitted it to himself—that those days he felt a bit let down.

But most days she was there.

Sometimes she even brought a sketch pad along

with her lunch and would sit on a park bench and work on things.

Decorating designs, he imagined.

He'd never tell her that every now and again he thought about taking a lunch outside and accidentally bumping into her. Maybe sitting right next to her on the same bench and eating.

That he'd been tempted to go back to her store and visit again after that day in the rain. There was something about Sarah that pulled at him. And if it wasn't for this entire marriage-to-make-partner nonsense, he'd never have talked to her again, other than a polite nod on the street. He had a career to build. He didn't have time for a relationship.

He'd grown up in a household where his parents tried to balance careers and a family—unfortunately the family part had suffered. When his grandmother, Dora, had come to live with them, things had been better. She'd always been there for him. But he still felt the lack.

He'd never had parents who came to all his football games, or to PTA meetings, or any of the other school activities parents typically attend. His mom had her business meetings, his dad had surgery, or rounds, or...

He swore that he'd build his career first, then think about a relationship, and maybe someday, a family. He'd make sure he'd reached a level at work where he could handle both. First step to that end was making partner. Then a few more years of establishing himself as one of the premier attorneys in Erie, then, maybe then he'd be ready for more.

By then Sarah would have found someone. A woman like her was going to be snapped up by someone.

He watched her surrounded by his colleagues.

Yeah, he'd meant what he'd said. Sarah Madison was a forever kind of woman. And the last thing Donovan needed was a woman with engagement rings on her mind.

Of course, she was wearing his engagement ring right now. He wasn't sure why he'd given her his grandmother's ring, why he'd told her the family story. But she'd gotten her wish; it was an engagement she could tell people about.

But it wouldn't last.

Next week she'd give the ring back and he'd return to his life, a partner in the firm before he hit thirty-five. That had always been his goal. Then he'd continue building his client base, and someday soon, maybe he'd be ready to look for a woman like Sarah.

He noticed she was looking at him. There was a hint of pleading in her eyes. He could tell she needed him. There was trust and confidence in that look. She trusted him to come running and was confident he could get her out of whatever she'd gotten herself into.

That she'd looked to him sent a surge of…something coursing through his veins. He wasn't sure what to call it, and wasn't about to try to define it.

He walked across the crowded room. He could see relief in Sarah's face the closer he drew.

"Sarah, I thought I was going to have to send a search party. I missed you," he said, draping his arm over her shoulder as if he belonged there. As if she belonged to him.

"Donovan, your friends have been generously offering to assist us with planning our wedding."

He could hear a faint tremor in her voice and resisted groaning. What on earth was Leland up to now?

"That's nice of you all, but I'm sure Sarah and I can manage."

"Manage?" Leland scoffed as he said the word. "Why, the poor girl was planning to wait until next year for her autumn wedding. We won't make either of you suffer like that. The girls suggested you marry here, at our home. You know, we're right on the lake, and Sarah's right, the trees will be more dazzling than any decoration. We thought we'd try for the second weekend in October. Her parents will be home by then, and it's a bit too early for even Erie to have a snowstorm, so that's perfect."

"But…" Donovan said. *But this was the last night of their engagement,* he wanted to say. But he couldn't say that. In fact, for a man who prided himself on being articulate, Donovan couldn't think of anything to say.

"I think what Donovan is trying to say is we just can't allow you all to put yourselves out like this on our behalves. But we thank you all for your kind offer."

"No, no. You're not robbing us of our fun. Oh, it's been so long since the family had a wedding. And I do so love weddings," Dorothy said.

"Oh, yes, we're all going to have so much fun," Leland said.

Fun.

That's not the word Donovan would use.

He looked at Sarah.

Judging by the expression on her face, he doubted it would be her word choice, either.

Chapter Four

Donovan to the rescue.

Like a knight in shining armor, he'd rescued her from wedding plans, giving vague, *Sarah and I will talk about it,* responses. She could have kissed him, but of course wouldn't, because though they were engaged, they weren't really.

Although…the thought of kissing Donovan wasn't overly upsetting. Sarah had a feeling that the only thing it would upset was her equilibrium. So she opted not to and instead settled for, "Thanks so much. I don't know how that happened, but I appreciate you getting me out of there. Next thing you know, they'd probably move past the wedding plans and right on to baby showers."

Donovan had been quiet, even for Donovan. His

only response was something akin to a grunt. So Sarah let silence wash between them as they made their goodbyes—well, actually Donovan made their goodbyes. Short, curt, *we're going now,* goodbyes. Sarah tossed in a few *thank you for the lovely evenings,* but this didn't seem to go over well with Donovan.

He practically tossed her into the car, then slammed her door behind her. He slammed his own when he got in on his side, then sped off.

Fine.

He was angry about the wedding plans.

Sarah went over and over the whole surreal scene, trying to decide what she could have done differently, and the only thing she could come up with was if she'd never gotten engaged to Donovan in the first place, then she wouldn't have ended up in that absurd predicament.

Well, let him be angry, she thought as they pulled up in front of her store.

"Thanks for the ride home," she said, prepared to make her escape. She tugged at the ring that weighed so heavily on her ever since he'd slid it into place.

It wasn't coming off.

Just one more complication in the world's most bizarre evening ever.

"The ring is stuck. I'll just soap it up when I get in and return it—"

"Leave it for now and go get your car," he said,

his voice and expression unreadable. "I'll follow you home. We have to talk about this."

"No," Sarah said in an automatic, flat response.

"No? You're not willing to talk about this…this situation we find ourselves in?"

"Yes, I'll talk to you about that, but no, you don't have to follow me home. We can talk at my office."

It was pride. She knew it was pride. But still, she wasn't telling Donovan that she was living in her office because she couldn't afford anything else. She hadn't told her parents, she wasn't telling him.

"Sarah, don't be silly. I'll follow you home. It's late. I don't like the thought of you going into your house unescorted anyway."

"I'm more than capable of taking care of myself, Donovan. I've been on my own a long time, and will be on my own again when this charade has ended. No matter what your office thinks, this isn't a real engagement. You have no obligation to me, other than settling that lawsuit."

"Sarah, what are you hiding?" he asked.

A sleeper-sofa in her office would be an accurate reply, but she settled for, "I don't know what you mean."

"Yes, you do. I've spent too many years reading people not to know when someone is being evasive. What is it about your home that you don't want me to know? Is it in a run-down section of town? You told me you had financial problems. I don't expect you to live in a mansion. I might be accused of a lot of things, but I don't think 'snob' is a word that people use to describe me. Is it?''

''No,'' she hastily assured him. ''I've never heard anyone say you were a snob. They don't even say a lot of things about you. At least not to me. Although, maybe it's because I'm your fiancée and they figure I'd defend you,'' she said, half-joking.

''Would you?'' he asked.

''Would I what?'' Following the twists and turns of Donovan's conversation was challenging. She could see why he was such a good attorney. He kept you on your toes as you tried to follow along.

''Would you defend me?''

The question sounded sincere. Did he care if she'd defend him or not?

''Sure I would,'' she said softly. ''You know, I think you're a much nicer guy than you let on, Donovan. I mean, either you're overbearing, thinking you have to see me safely home, or you're sweet. I'm voting for sweet.''

''I'm not sweet.'' He scowled as he said the word, as if the mere sound of it was offensive to his sensibilities.

Sarah resisted telling him that his reaction was even sweeter than his wanting to take care of her.

''Okay, if you say so,'' she said, trying to placate

him. ''But I'm not taking you to my home, so if you want to talk, we'll talk in my office.''

She opened her car door, ready to leave the car and the absurd argument behind.

Donovan reached past her and pulled her door shut. ''Never mind, we'll talk at my house, and I'll bring you back when we're done.''

He put the car into drive and swung around Perry Square and down State Street.

''Donovan, I don't want to put you out,'' she said. ''Just drop me off and let me get my car, I'll follow you. That way you won't have to bring me home later.''

''You're not putting me out. Like I said during our crash-course on each other, I've got a condo on the bay. It will only take a few minutes to take you back later.''

They lapsed back into silence.

Sarah should have just told him she was living out of her office. But she knew he'd lecture her, just like her parents would lecture her if they knew.

Well, she didn't need any lectures. She was a big girl. And she knew that things would be tight when she decided to go into business for herself. She knew it, and she accepted the consequences.

Donovan's car stopped. His was the last condo, right at the edge of the water.

She should have guessed. Only the best would do

for Elias Donovan. She silently rolled his first name around in her mouth. She liked the feel of it. Elias.

Yes, she liked it, though with the mood he was in, she wasn't going to risk using it. She'd just think it. Elias.

He hit a garage door opener and slid his car into the garage.

"Come on," he said gruffly. He got out of the car and led her to the door and opened it.

Sarah planted her feet, for some reason unwilling to go into Donovan's home. She wasn't sure why. It wasn't as if she was afraid of him. No, just the opposite. She trusted him. That's why she'd made the appointment with him instead of one of the other attorneys at his firm.

She didn't understand that feeling of trust. It wasn't as if she really knew him. Other than that day he'd rushed into her box-littered store, she hadn't said more than two words to him. Even then they hadn't really conversed. But there was something about Elias Donovan that made her feel...safe. Her father would have a lot to say about trusting a man based on an unsubstantiated feeling, but Sarah couldn't help it. She trusted Donovan.

But trust or not, she needed to keep what was between them strictly business. Meeting in his office, messy as it was, or hers, that was business. Coming into his home...well, it wasn't.

"Really, Donovan, this isn't necessary, and...and

I have to get up early, so I need to get home to bed now. You can stop by my office tomorrow afternoon.''

His hand was planted firmly in the small of her back as he practically pushed her into his kitchen. "Liar. Tomorrow is Sunday, so there's no need to make it an early evening. You can sleep in.''

"I have work to do. I'm trying to get my company off the ground, remember? I don't take weekends off.''

"Well, you can take one morning off and sleep in. We need to talk now and figure out what to do.'' He flipped on the main light.

The kitchen was…sleek. That was the right word for it. Chrome fixtures. Black countertops. White cupboards. And an entire wall that was pretty much glass, overlooking the bay. Even in the dark, little lights dotted the water. Boats, or maybe buoys?

Sarah wasn't sure.

What she was sure of was that if she'd designed Donovan's kitchen, she'd have done it like this. The style suited him.

He had a glass table set right in front of the huge expanse of windows and he pulled out one of the two chairs. "Sit.''

"I—'' Sarah was about to argue, but one look at Donovan's expression convinced her it was best to get this over with. "Thank you.''

"Do you want something to drink?'' he asked.

"No. I'm fine."

"I have some wine open," he said, as if he didn't hear her negative response. He poured two glasses and brought them to the table. "Here."

"Thank you."

"Now, about these wedding plans?"

"Donovan, I'm so sorry. I don't know how it happened. One minute I was talking to Hanni, Brigitta and Liesl, and the next thing I knew Mr. and Mrs. Wagner were there, and everyone was busy planning an October wedding."

She took a sip of the wine. She wasn't an expert, but knew this was no twist-top variety. It was smooth and warm.

"It was as if half of your office suddenly appeared. They were talking wedding gowns and bridesmaids before I got a chance to say anything."

She took another sip of wine. "We'll have to have a public breakup and the sooner the better. They were talking about calling around for tents on Monday. I don't want any deposits or anything put on things. It's just throwing money away."

"Or..."

"Or?" she repeated.

"Or we could do it."

"Do what?"

"We could get married."

Shell-shocked.

Donovan studied his newly acquired fiancée and realized that "shell-shocked" was the only appropriate phrase to describe Sarah's expression as he said the words.

When she roused herself to move, she drained her entire glass of wine.

He felt almost as surprised as she looked when he heard the words come out of his mouth, but as soon as they had, he knew he was on to something.

He got up and brought the bottle back to the table and as he poured, he said, "There would be advantages to both of us."

"You've got to be out of your mind." Sarah took another hefty gulp of wine.

"No, listen. A fiancée was good, but a wife would be even better for my career. Not just *my* career. Yours as well. Marrying me would give you entry into a group of people who by their social status are ever so much more inclined to use an interior decorator, so there's a financial benefit for you."

"And I believe there's a word for women who would take this kind of a step for money."

"Smart. That's the word. After all, for centuries marriages were arranged not for love, but for social and economic reasons."

Sarah shook her head. "Not anymore. People have learned that marriage must be based on love if it's going to work. The rest...well, if you love the other person, you can make the rest work."

"In some places they still arrange marriages for

social and economic reasons," he pointed out. He didn't say that the last thing he'd ever want was to be tied to a woman he didn't love any more than she wanted to be tied to a loveless marriage.

But this wouldn't be a real marriage, he assured himself. It would just be a temporary sham. A partnership, nothing more.

"Other countries might still do that sort of thing. But not here. And not me. I think I'm ready to go home now."

She started to stand, but Donovan took her hand and pulled her back into her seat. His fingers brushed the ring—his ring—on her hand. An unexpected feeling of…well, something flooded his body. He wasn't sure what it was, but he did know he liked the way the ring felt on Sarah's hand.

She pulled her hand away, as if he had some killer case of childhood cooties. Donovan let it go, satisfied that she was still sitting.

"Hear me out," he said. "Neither of us are attached to anyone, so who would we hurt? No one. We'll sign a prenup. Either of us can ask to dissolve the union with no penalties. What was mine before the wedding remains mine. What was yours, remains yours. We'll split the living expenses. No one loses anything, and we both gain a lot."

"I—"

"It's perfect. I don't know why I didn't think of

it before. A wife will work so much better than a fiancée.''

''Donovan, I don't think so.''

''Why? This wouldn't be a marriage. Believe it or not, I have plans to marry someday for love. But I'm not in the position to do it now, and neither are you. This isn't marriage in the traditional sense. It's more of a partnership. A business partnership. One that will allow both of us to reap the benefits, and then walk away friends when it's over.''

''Friends? Is that what we are?'' she asked.

''Not yet, maybe. But we're friendly, and I think, given time—''

''And a marriage.''

''—and a marriage, we could be very good friends.''

''Donovan, the engagement idea was crazy, but I went along with it because, like you said, I didn't think it would hurt anyone, and it would help both of us out. But this? What you're proposing? It's never going to work.''

''The only people that could be hurt is us…and since we're not in love, we're safe. This is a marriage-of-convenience. As I said, we'll draw up a prenup and make it all nice and legal. And when the marriage has served its purpose, we'll both walk away friends, and better off. Your business will have improved, and I'll be a partner in the firm, just like I deserve.''

''But…'' Sarah's voice trailed off. She finished her

glass of wine. "Donovan. It all sounds logical when you say it like that, but I'm sure there's something we're not thinking of. Some complication that will crop up and bite us in the butt."

"Sarah, I'll watch your backside, if you watch mine." He meant it to sound flip, but it simply reminded him that watching Sarah's backside would be no hardship. He'd been watching it for a long time…longer than this fake engagement.

"Donovan," she said, her voice laced with exasperation.

"That's not much of an argument."

"You're the lawyer, arguing is your forte, not mine."

"So don't argue. Say yes. Say you'll marry me."

"And make you the happiest man in the world?" she asked, sarcasm touching every word.

"It would make me happy, Sarah. I think we could be good for each other. If I didn't, I would never suggest this."

"If I were to say yes, how would we work it?"

"We'd start with an iron-clad prenuptial agreement. What's yours is yours, what's mine is mine. A separate household account we both contribute to, and—"

He cut himself off as Sarah yawned. "Listen, don't say yes or no. Sleep on it."

She nodded. "I think sleeping on it is a good idea

for both of us. Tomorrow you'll come to your senses.''

''I never lost my senses, but maybe you'll find yours overnight. Come on, I'll take you home.''

''Back to the store,'' she corrected.

''Home. It's too late, you're too tired, and you've had two glasses of wine here, plus who knows how many at the party.''

He paused, studying her. Yes, there was something she wasn't telling him. ''Why don't you want me to see your home?''

''Donovan, please don't start this again.'' She sighed an exasperated sigh and stared out the window. She seemed fascinated by the view, even though it was dark.

Donovan could understand that. Even at night lights dotted the bay, and the stars loomed big and bright over the peninsula across the water.

The view was why he'd bought the condo. But Sarah was trying to hide something by watching it. He reached across the table, took her chin lightly in his hand and turned her head until she faced him. ''Sarah, why?''

Her eyes met his. ''If you take me to the store, I won't be driving anywhere else. The store is my home.''

''What?''

''I have a pullout sofa in the office. I told you money was tight. I was waiting, saving for a place of my own. And if the Rat had paid, I'd have one, but he didn't, so I'm still waiting.''

He might not have been through the entire store, but Donovan knew it was one of the smaller buildings on the square. She was living in it? ''You can't live in your office.''

''No? You think a fake engagement gives you the right to tell me what to do?'' she asked, bristling.

''Yes, I do. You can't live in your store.'' He paused a moment, trying to decide how to handle this new twist.

Ever since Sarah had walked into his office there had been a series of unexpected twists and turns. He was getting good at keeping up.

''You'll sleep here,'' he said before he'd hardly registered making a decision.

''Oh, no.'' She shook her head with such force that red curls sprang free from their confines, hanging there, begging to be tucked back in.

As much as he'd like to tuck it, Donovan was wise enough to realize Sarah wouldn't appreciate it, so he kept his hands firmly planted on the table. ''I have a spare room.''

''Good for you.'' She started to stand. ''I'm leaving. It's just a short walk home.''

Donovan sprang from his chair and stood in front of her, blocking the way. ''Sarah, this isn't open to debate.''

''Oh, no? Even if I was to agree to your stupid

plan and marry you, I wouldn't let you boss me around. And if you get me that money from Ratgaz, then I'll be in my own apartment soon enough.''

He changed his approach, forcing himself to soften his tone. ''Just for tonight, stay here.''

''No, I—''

''Please?'' he asked, surprising himself, and obviously Sarah as well. She simply stared at him.

What was going on in her mind as she studied him so intently? What did she see?

Donovan knew what he saw. An independent, determined, beautiful woman.

''In a guest room, right?'' she finally asked softly.

''Yes.''

''Just for tonight?''

''For tonight,'' he agreed, omitting the *just*.

He didn't like the idea of Sarah sleeping in her office, and if they were going to be married, even if it was only for convenience, it made sense for her to move in with him. He had plenty of room, and her staying here would only add to the realism of their being a couple.

''All right,'' she finally said.

Chapter Five

Sarah froze midstretch. Something was wrong.

Slowly she pried her eyes open and took in her surroundings. She wasn't in her own sleeper-sofa bed. She wasn't in her office. She was—

The realization slowly sank in. She was in Donovan's guest-room bed, wearing his old T-shirt. It was soft and a little thin from too many washings. It smelled like him. Warm and spicy. He smelled so much different from the persona he put forward.

The Iceman...that's what they called him. And yet, he didn't seem icy at all. Last night, when she'd confessed she lived in her office...well, despite the fact he was overbearing and heavy-handed when he'd insisted she stay with him, he seemed concerned.

The concern part was touching. And when he'd

stopped demanding and simply said the word *please* she hadn't been able to say no. Maybe she'd had too much wine after all?

Well, pleased or not, she didn't plan to stay here again. She was too exhausted last night to put up a fight was all. And she had a lot to fight about.

Imagine, he wanted to make this fake engagement into a fake marriage.

Sarah might be desperate, but she didn't think she'd sunk that low yet.

She toyed with the ring—his grandmother's ring—that he'd put on her finger. She'd have to give it back today and tell him in no uncertain terms that she wasn't entering into a marriage-of-convenience. She had more pride than that.

Of course, he could really use her help in securing that partnership. Donovan didn't strike her as the type to ask for help...ever. And yet, he'd asked. He needed her.

Plus, he'd framed the proposal in such a way that she'd benefit from it, but when it came down to brass tacks, he needed her more and he'd asked for her help.

Sarah groaned. How could she say no? He deserved to be a partner, and it was unfair to make that reward conditional on something like marriage. After all, you couldn't make yourself fall in love.

But how could she say yes?

How could she marry a man who didn't love her, and who she didn't love?

Unable to answer the question, Sarah got out of bed, headed into the guest room's bathroom.

She almost groaned with the pleasure of it all. It was so nice to get a shower without having to go to the Y. She took a long, luxurious, private shower. The only thing that would have made it better was if she'd had clean clothes, she thought as she slid back into last night's cocktail dress.

She spent a few minutes finger combing her damp curls, and applying what little makeup she'd brought in her small clutch purse. Feeling at least slightly presentable, she went out to the living room in search of her soon-to-be ex-fiancée.

Donovan was sprawled on the couch. She studied him a moment. He seemed more approachable this morning. Maybe it was his outfit. A polo shirt, well-worn jeans, and plain white socks. His feet were propped on the coffee table as he scribbled on the pad on his lap.

His hair wasn't quite as perfect, either. That one erstwhile tiny strand of hair drifted down on his forehead. He had on glasses.

She didn't know he wore glasses. They looked sexy on him. That wasn't fair. He shouldn't look sexier with glasses on, but he did.

Realizing she could easily stand in the doorway and

continue just drinking in the sight of him, Sarah forced herself to move.

"Good morning," she said.

He looked up and slipped his glasses off. "Sorry, I didn't hear you come in. I trust you slept all right?"

Sarah nodded. "Any chance you can give me a ride home?"

She wanted to go home, go back to her normal, non-Donovan life. She wanted to forget about fake engagements, and marriages-of-convenience. And most especially, she wanted to forget that Donovan looked sexy in—and out of—glasses.

"I thought we'd go out for breakfast." He set the pad and his glasses on the table, and stood, moving toward her.

Sarah took a small step backward, keeping a nice, comfortable distance between them. "I'd rather not. I mean, I don't think I'm really dressed for a Sunday morning breakfast."

"We could stop at your place so you can change first."

"Thanks, but I think it's time I—"

"Please. I'd really like to pick up last night's conversation."

"Donovan. About that—"

He held up a hand, as if he could physically hold off her protests. "No. Don't say anything until you hear me out."

"I don't think it will do any good." There was no way she could marry a man she didn't love.

"Come on," he grabbed the tablet as he walked toward the door. "Let's go."

Sensing she wasn't going to win this one, Sarah just nodded. She'd go out to breakfast with him, listen to his spiel, and then politely refuse. She'd return his ring and get back to normal.

The drive to her store was a silent one. He parked right out front, and Sarah opened the door and called over her shoulder, "I'll be right out," as she hurried into the safety of her store.

Donovan was as thick as a brick and didn't take the hint, but followed her into the store.

"You can have a seat out here and wait," she said, indicating the nice chairs she'd used to decorate the outer office.

He obviously didn't appreciate her efforts. Rather than trying one, he said, "Show me where you sleep," in that bossy way of his.

"Like I told you, in my office."

He strode ahead of her and walked through the open door into her inner office.

"On that?" he asked, nodding at the sofa.

"It's a sleeper-sofa. It's not that bad." She didn't mention the huge bump in the middle. No matter what way she slept, some part of her body ended up on it and aching the next day.

He opened the door to the bathroom. "There's no shower."

"I work out at the Y every morning, so I just shower there. It's very economical, and it certainly motivates me to work out every day."

He shook his head. "You can't keep living like this."

"I won't much longer. That is, if you're a good enough lawyer to get the money from the Rat," she said.

It was a challenge…she'd thrown down the gauntlet.

Donovan wasted no time picking it up. "I'm good, more than good enough. I've looked through your material, and you have a case. I'll win. But still, it could take time."

"Then, I'll just tough it out." She shrugged, trying to act as if it didn't matter, even as she internally groaned. She'd never admit it to Donovan, but this situation wasn't exactly as comfortable as she tried to pretend.

Last night, in Donovan's guest bed, she'd enjoyed the first good sleep she'd had since she'd opened By Design.

He was still shaking his head. "Get changed. I have a couple ideas."

"Donovan," she protested.

"Now." He left her office and shut the door.

Of all the dictorial, overbearing, sure-he-knew-what-was-right, but didn't-have-a-clue-about-anything men. It would serve him right if she simply let him chill out there all day.

Knowing he was just on the other side of the door gave Sarah shivers as she climbed out of her dress and grabbed a pair of jeans and a bright orange shirt from her wardrobe. She was just buttoning the jeans when the door flew open.

"Hey!" Sarah cried.

"It's just me, sweetums," a gray-haired lady with a ready smile and a hint of the South in her voice said.

Pearly Gates worked a few storefronts down at Snips And Snaps Beauty Salon. She'd *adopted* Sarah as her personal pet project. She'd sent a few of her friends over for small decorating jobs, and generally turned up whenever Sarah needed an ear or a shoulder.

Today Sarah didn't really want either. She just wanted to "break up" with Donovan and get back to her life.

Obviously Pearly didn't realize that because she took a seat on the sofa without waiting for an invitation. "I stopped at the store to pick up some perm rods at the salon. I'm giving my friend Justine a perm today, although, between you and me, she would look better without one. But that's neither here nor there. As I left the salon, I saw Donovan sitting bold as brass in a chair in front of the window. And of course,

I said to myself, *Now what would Donovan be doin'
at Sarah Jane's first thing on a Sunday morning?* And
me, being me, I couldn't wait until tomorrow to ask
you, so I just came right in to find out.''

Sarah sat next to Pearly and said, ''He's—''

The older woman interrupted her. ''And do be
careful what you tell me because, much as I'd like
the dirt, you and I both know I'm a horrible gossip,
and will have to spread your news up and down the
four corners of Perry Square.''

Sarah tried to think quick, deciding what version
of the truth to tell Pearly. ''Well, you see, we're engaged, sort of.''

''Sort of? I had an aunt once who was *sort of* engaged. After that, she was *sort of* pregnant, and the
weddin' never did take place. But the birthin' did.
That would be my cousin Lerlene. There've been
times I wish I could make her *sort of* a cousin, because of her personality…which is in and of itself less
than legitimate. I've had more interesting conversations with a turnip. So, I'll be needin' you to explain
this *sort of* engagement.''

''Well, we are engaged, but things are—'' Sarah
tried to think of whatever story they'd be putting out
''—they're not going well, and I was thinking about
breaking things off. That's why Donovan's here this
morning. We're going out to breakfast to discuss our
options.''

''Now, I could ask you how it is you and Donovan

have been carrying on here on the Square without me, Josie, Libby or even that needle-pushing woman Mabel finding out, but I won't. What I will tell you is that love shouldn't be forsaken just 'cause it ain't *going well*. That's what a commitment is about. Sticking out the *not going well* times and waiting until the *going better* ones.''

''But sometimes you just have to cut your losses,'' Sarah said.

This was certainly one of those times. She'd signed on to be a fiancée for one night, and it was the next day, and she was still a fiancée. Absentmindedly, she twisted the ring on her finger.

''Cut your losses? Now, that sounds like a lawyer talkin' there. Lawyers. They're a rather clueless species. Add to that Donovan's a man, well, it's even worse. Clueless as a pig in a pen. That's why God created women…to clue them in. And I don't think you're some wishy-washy woman who gives up at the first sign of hardship. Why did I ever tell you about my cousin Lerlene?''

Sarah sensed a long story coming—long stories were Pearly's forte. Maybe she should try to stop her right here since Donovan was still sitting in the other room. But, since she didn't especially want to face Donovan, she said, ''You just mentioned that Lerlene's not a great conversationalist.''

''Well, I was right about that. Like I said, turnips

were more interesting. But somehow, years ago, she managed to capture a beau. His name was Trubald.''

"Trubald?" Sarah repeated.

Pearly bristled. "It's a good name. His granddad Trubald was a soldier and that's who he was named after. Anyway, he lost his leg.''

"Trubald's grandfather lost his leg in a war?'' Sarah asked.

"No, Trubald.''

"Oh, how tragic. That must have been hard for him to deal with. How did it happen?''

Pearly skooched half a cushion closer, and her voice lowered, as if she were telling some State secret. "Well, the way it was told to me was, he was out drinking one night, and just lost it. No one ever quite figured out how you just lose a leg, but somehow Trubald did it, and no one ever saw hide nor hair of it again.''

"He's lucky he didn't bleed to death,'' Sarah said, trying to imagine being so drunk you could lose a leg and not know how.

"Now, why on earth would losing a prosthetic limb make you bleed to death?'' Pearly lightly tapped Sarah's forehead. "Keep up, girl. He'd had that peg leg since he was seventeen and lost his real leg in a fluke racin' accident.''

Sarah wasn't going to ask what a fluke racing accident was. She just wanted to get out of here, so she wasn't going to ask.

She wasn't.

But Pearly just sat there, obviously waiting for her to ask, and despite her best intentions she couldn't disappoint Pearly. So she asked, "Fluke racing accident?"

Pearly beamed. "Yep. Trubald, he was racin' his brother Truck—who, before you ask, was really named Truman, but seeing as he looked more like a truck than a Truman, well, Truck was the name he went by. And he was racin' Trubald that day when Trubald lost his leg. Only it wasn't a fair race. Truck was in an auto and Trubald wasn't. Trubald, he slipped and Truck ran over his leg. So Trubald got that fake one, and years later got drunk one night and lost it."

Pearly paused and sucked in a quick breath. Sarah was waiting for it, ready to jump and try to get out of this story, but years of telling long-winded stories had made Pearly an expert on breathing without giving up the floor. Before Sarah could get a word in edgewise, Pearly was back at it.

"Well, my cousin Lerlene said she wasn't marrying no man who drank so much he lost a leg, and she broke off their engagement. A couple years later, Trubald, he laid off the drink, got a new leg and a new fiancée and Lerlene's one chance at love limped off to a marriage that's still strong today."

"Oh." Sarah didn't know what to say, didn't know what the point of the story was and was terrified to ask because Pearly didn't seem to be able to give monosyllabic responses.

Even though she wanted to avoid the confrontation with Donovan, she knew she had to face him eventually and was thinking confronting him was easier than making sense of Pearly's stories.

"Now do you see what I mean?" Pearly demanded.

"Yes," Sarah said decisively, even though she didn't truly have a clue.

"What?"

"Umm... Don't get drunk and lose your leg or you'll lose your fiancée?" she tried.

"No, you addlebrained girl," Pearly said, giving Sarah another soft thwap on the forehead. "Now, I know you have more brains that turnip-talking Lerlene, but brains doesn't have a thing to do with love. You can't just throw love away because things are tough. You work it out. If Lerlene had worked it out with Trubald, she might not be a bitter, single, turnip-talkin' woman today."

"Single isn't bad," Sarah pointed out.

She was happy in her singleness. Happy to be able to come and go as she pleased, not to have to answer to anyone else. She could live in her office, sleep on her lumpy sleeper-sofa if she wanted to—not that she wanted to—but the point was, she didn't have to answer to anyone.

Donovan could storm into her office and bluster

about how she chose to live all he wanted, but because she was single, and single-minded in her goals, she didn't have to listen. She was going to make By Design a success, and was willing to tough it out the first year in order to do it.

"No. I'm the poster child for the slogan Single Isn't Bad," Pearly said. "I'm happy in my singleness. But pinin' away for something you threw away is bad. Letting go without fighting for a relationship is worse."

"But—"

Pearly stood. "Gotta go. You've got a man waitin' to take you to breakfast," Pearly added as she unceremoniously, and uncharacteristically, left Sarah's office without another word. She closed the door behind her with a small bang.

Sarah sat, trying to sort out everything Pearly had said. If she and Donovan had a *real* engagement, if they *really* loved each other, she wouldn't give up. She would willingly fight for it—for them. But they didn't. This was just an engagement-of-convenience, a short-term contract between them. There was nothing to fight for. Or so she tried to tell herself as she went out to meet Donovan.

Donovan stared at the woman across the breakfast table from him. All those days he'd watched her eat her lunches in the park, he'd never imagined he'd be sitting at a table eating with her, much less pressing her to actually marry him.

"But, just stop and consider the advantages," he said, pressing his point.

"You'd make partner." She speared a piece of her pancake.

Donovan swallowed a quick gulp of coffee. He needed all the energy and caffeine his body could absorb. Sarah was a well-matched opponent.

"Yes," he said slowly. "And that's my reason for this union. But there are reasons for you to agree as well."

She nodded, "Moving in the *right* circles for my business."

"Yes. But beyond that, there's the small matter of a roof over your head."

She lived in her office.

The thought had been eating at him since last night. Someone like Sarah deserved the best of everything, not some lumpy couch and a bathroom that didn't even have a shower. She went to the Y every day.

"I have a roof over my head." She had this stubborn little expression on her face.

Donovan wasn't about to tell her that she looked cute. Sort of like an Irish setter pretending to be a pit bull. He was pretty sure she wouldn't appreciate the dog analogy. But her hair was the exact same shade as the dog his grandmother had owned.

"I'm talking about a home, not just a roof. And living in your office isn't a home."

"Let's get the semantics straight—you're talking about a house. A home is a place where a family lives, and you're not proposing we become a family. This is a business proposal."

She wasn't eating her pancakes any longer, merely pushing the pieces through the syrup. He wondered if she ate right. She was skinny enough to make him wonder if she was skipping meals to save money. Well, as soon as he got her home, he'd be sure she ate healthily and regularly.

"Fine," he said, willing to agree to her point. "It might not be a home, but you'd have a real house, a real bed and a real shower. I know I first suggested a household account, splitting the bills, but that doesn't seem right."

"I can pay my own way," she practically growled.

"But, I'll be the one benefiting the most from this arrangement, so it's only fair that I shoulder the greater part of the financial burden."

No way was he going to take her money. He had plenty and she was homeless, practically starving herself.

Okay, that might be overstating the facts, but he wasn't taking her money.

"I'm no one's burden," Sarah muttered.

"That's not what I meant. Listen, I'm already paying all the bills at my place. Your moving in won't add any expense.''

''Food.''

Oh, if he had his way, his food bill would go way up. The more he thought about it, the more skinny she seemed. He'd have to find a way to get her a physical. Maybe she'd made herself sick.

''Fine,'' he readily agreed. ''You pay for half the food.''

He'd see to it she ate more than half the food anyway. He was a pretty decent cook, thanks to his grandma Dora. Although it had been years since he'd done much of it. There just didn't seem to be a point in cooking for just himself. But he'd enjoy cooking for Sarah.

He'd start with his grandmother's beef stew and dumplings. No one could resist that. And if he did say so himself, his dumplings were lighter than even his grandmother's had been.

He realized Sarah was still talking money as he daydreamed about feeding her.

''I pay for all the food,'' she said.

''Fine.'' He picked up his legal pad and scribbled a note. ''I'll add that to our prenup. You'll live at my house, I'll continue paying all the bills associated with it, and you'll shoulder the grocery bill. We could go shopping Saturday mornings. That gives me the day to get meals for the following week prepared.''

He scribbled another note to himself, "I should have mentioned, I'll cook."

"You cook?" she asked, sounding way too surprised.

"Wait until you try something I've made. That hint of skepticism in your voice will disappear immediately."

"I can't see The Iceman puttering around in his kitchen." She shook her head, trying to look serious, but he saw the spark of humor in those light gray eyes.

"There's a lot about me you don't know," he said, and quickly reminded himself there was a lot about her he didn't know either.

Donovan realized he was excited about discovering all those unknown things. Why?

This was business, he reminded himself. The only reason he was worried about her eating habits was it wouldn't do to have a sick wife.

"Hey, wait a minute," Sarah said hastily. "I just need to be clear on what we're doing. We're talking theoretically. I'm not agreeing to anything."

Sensing that he'd pushed far enough for the moment, Donovan switched tactics. "So what did Pearly want?"

Sarah looked a little surprised by his change of subject and answered cautiously. "She wanted to know what you were doing at my place on a Sunday morning."

"Stop playing with your pancakes and eat them. You're all skin and bones," he said. He couldn't stand seeing her move that one slice through the syrup puddle again.

Satisfied when she ate the bite, and hoping to keep her unsettled, he asked, "So what did you tell Pearly?"

Sarah finished chewing and said, "What we agreed. That we were engaged, and things weren't going well."

Sarah smiled...the first genuine smile he'd seen all day. Donovan wouldn't have admitted it to anyone, but he liked her smile.

Who was he kidding? He liked the way she looked when she smiled, when she frowned, and he'd especially liked the way she'd looked when she turned to him last night to rescue her from his wedding-planner colleagues.

Donovan simply liked looking at her.

Her hair was a soft reddish tint, and that light sprinkling of freckles across her nose...he wondered how many freckles there were. He'd like to count and see, but he couldn't imagine she'd stand for that.

Her grayish-blue eyes met his without flinching. She stood up to him, challenged him left and right. Not many people did that. Most people were intimidated by him, and that's the way he liked it.

But he was glad Sarah wasn't. Why that was, he

wasn't sure. He forced himself to concentrate on what she was saying.

"...and then she said that her cousin Lerlene should have stuck by the missing-leg Trubald. Oh, I made a mess of that story. I don't think anyone can tell a Pearly story and make the moral work out quite the way she does. But her point was, you stick it out through the rough times, if you really love someone. Of course, I couldn't tell her we don't."

"Right. This isn't a love match. This is business," he said, reminding himself more than Sarah.

"But I didn't tell her that."

"So to get back to our original subject, about marrying me."

"Donovan, are you always this persistent?" Sarah asked.

He noted she'd finished her pancakes and pushed his plate of untouched hash browns her way. "Try these. I'm full and can't eat another bite, but it's a shame to waste them. They're delicious."

"You're changing the subject again. I asked if you were always this persistent," she repeated, even as she obligingly took a bite. "Oh, these are good."

"Yes," he answered, and smiled as she took a second bite. "Being persistent is why I'm such a good attorney and deserve this promotion. A promotion that might be in jeopardy if you break things off."

"But you said you just needed a fiancée for the night," she reminded him.

Donovan took a sip of coffee, using the moment to come up with an answer.

"I thought that would be enough, but after watching how Leland and everyone jumped on the idea of us truly getting married, well, I think breaking things off could mean I'm out of the running."

"It's not fair for you to put your promotion all on me," she said softly.

"It's not fair that a partnership I deserve depends on whether or not I'm in a relationship. It's not fair that Ratgaz owes you money and hasn't paid. It's not fair that a talented decorator is living at her office."

"How do you know I'm talented?" she asked abruptly.

"I saw what you did with your office and—"

"And?"

"And I paid a visit to Ratgaz's office last week after our meeting. I saw what you did there. You're very talented. I have no doubt that you're going to make it, as soon as others realize it."

He didn't add he'd met the man and that it was all he could do not to throw a punch at him. He hated Ratgaz on sight for what he'd put Sarah through. And when he saw what a wonderful job she'd done decorating the offices—an entire floor of offices, plus the reception area—he hated Ratgaz even more.

Sarah hadn't responded, so he added, "You're going to make it if you can keep your business afloat until then. That's what I'm offering you, a chance to stay afloat while you build your clientele.''

"Donovan, this will never work.'' She shook her head, her hair swaying to and fro. ''Someone will end up hurt.''

"No. We'll nail everything down before the wedding. We'll leave nothing to chance. As long as we've got it all in black and white, there's no way either of us will be hurt.'' He touched the legal pad. ''That's what I've been working on.''

"But—''

"Listen, I've already started. 'Whereas, the parties are anticipating marriage to each other; Whereas, in anticipation of their intended marriage, the parties desire to express in writing their agreement—'''

Sarah cut him off. "Oh, please not legalese. Just tell me in English what you'd have it say.''

Donovan chuckled. Maybe he needed to hang out with more nonlawyer friends in order to remember how real people talked.

"What it says, in essence, is what's mine is mine, what's yours is yours, now and after the marriage ends. While I waited at your office, I tossed in a few other ideas. We'll live at my place, not yours.''

He realized that statement came out hard and sounded rather cold, so he offered her a smile to soften it.

"Donovan, was that a joke?'' Sarah asked, and

thwacked her hand on her chest. "Oh, be still my heart. The Iceman is joking?"

Donovan found himself smiling back at her. "Don't mock me before lunch. I can be dangerous."

She studied him for a long, silent minute. "I'm beginning to suspect you want people to believe that. I don't know that I necessarily believe it's so."

Donovan felt…exposed.

Exposed. That was the word. As if Sarah knew things about him that even he didn't know. And he didn't like it. He wasn't used to it. He wasn't going to put up with it.

"You should," he said, giving her his fiercest glare—the one guaranteed to make other attorneys or witnesses cower in their shoes.

She smiled a smile that said she wasn't buying it. Flustered, he cleared his throat and consulted his legal pad. "Back to business. Some of this we've already covered. Such as, I'll continue to pay the bills I've normally paid."

"Anything over and beyond that is mine," Sarah said.

"I don't know that we need all that in the prenup, though," he added.

"You said it yourself, we need everything in it. If we cover everything in the prenup there shouldn't be any hurt feelings when everything ends," she pointed out.

"Fine." He scratched a note. "I've also provided

that when we want to dissolve the marriage—either one of us, or both of us—that it will be ended in the most expedient means possible. There will be no spousal support. And child support isn't in question since we're not having any—'' He stopped.

Sex. They weren't going to have any sex. That's what he had been about to say, but as he looked at Sarah he realized that it would be impossible to have sex with her, ever. Making love. That's what it would be with a woman like Sarah. Not that they were going to do that, either.

"Children," she filled in for him.

"What?" His mind was still foggy with the images of making love with Sarah.

"There won't be any children," she repeated. "Since this isn't going to be a, well, physical sort of marriage, there's no question of child support."

"Right." He felt suddenly very warm, and took a sip of his lukewarm coffee hoping to cool himself off. Where was their waitress? "Can you think of anything you'd want included?"

"We'd have to have it in writing that neither of us would ever disclose the actual nature of our marriage."

"That's good." He scribbled a note. "I can draw this up Monday."

Softly, Sarah said, "I haven't agreed. This is all hypothetical."

Donovan dropped the pen. "Say yes. Don't think about it, don't analyze it, just say yes."

"But talking about a prenup is easy. Going through with a marriage-of-convenience…I just don't think I have it in me, Donovan. Much as I'd like to help you, I just don't think I can."

"Sarah, this might not be a traditional marriage agreement, but I think we both have something to offer the other. And, I'll be honest, I need you."

She was quiet for a moment, and Donovan was sure she was going to say no. He felt a wave of…what was that feeling? Disappointment?

Maybe.

But not because he'd wanted to marry her for personal reasons. No. His need for Sarah was business. Purely business.

He wanted to build a flourishing career, to make partner and then to settle back and find a wife, have a family, when he had time for them.

And yet, if he was looking for a woman…

He gazed at the woman across the table from him. Yes, if he was looking now, he wouldn't look far.

"Yes," she said.

"Pardon?"

"Yes, I'll marry you."

Chapter Six

What on earth had she done?

What had she been thinking?

What could possibly have been in those delicious pancakes that would make her agree to such a thing? No, it wasn't the pancakes, it was probably the hash browns Donovan had insisted she eat.

Sarah kept asking herself these questions as she sat at her desk the next day pretending to work. But unfortunately she had yet to answer herself.

That was the problem with one-sided conversations…you never got a second opinion. And since this entire situation was hush-hush, just between her and Donovan, the only second-opinion she could get was his, and she didn't think that was going to help. He'd been the one to talk her into it in the first place. She didn't have a clue why she'd agreed to make her engagement-of-convenience a marriage-of-convenience.

The only bright spot was it meant that Donovan was very persuasive: a good quality in a lawyer who was handling her case against the Rat.

Sarah looked at her appointment book, and rather than feel thrilled at seeing so many new appointments, she felt decidedly morose.

She felt like a fake.

As if she wasn't good enough to make a go of the decorating business without Donovan's help.

She could have asked for her parents' help and achieved the same end. But she hadn't. She'd wanted to do this on her own. She'd wanted to be able to look at the business she'd built, and know it was achieved through merit, not through handouts.

Leland Wagner himself had called and was her last appointment today, and just one of five appointments for the week made by people she'd met at the party.

Darn.

No. She refused to think that way. Donovan might have introduced her, but she'd get the jobs on her own merit, and she'd get more because of them.

She heard the buzzer that indicated someone had entered the building. As she walked into her outer room, she tried to work up some enthusiasm, but she didn't feel it was all that convincing.

"Hello, Mr. Wagner," she said to the gray-haired man she'd met just Saturday night.

Saturday.

She found it hard to believe that things had happened so fast since then. Just a weekend separated today from then. How could so many things change so fast?

"Hello, my dear," he said with a small nod of his head.

"Would you like to have a seat?" She indicated a chair.

He waited for her to sit and then took his seat as well. "First, I'd like a chance to congratulate you again, Sarah. We were so delighted to meet you at our party and were even more pleased to hear your and Donovan's news."

"About that," she said. "I feel a bit guilty. After all, it was your anniversary party, and yet, some of the focus shifted to Donovan and myself."

"What could be lovelier than celebrating a lifetime of happiness by announcing the beginning of someone else's relationship? Truly, it was our pleasure. And Dorothy is so excited about helping with your wedding."

Mrs. Wagner had called earlier and said she couldn't wait to start planning the wedding. Her excitement only served to make Sarah feel more guilty.

"But that's not why I'm here today," he continued. "I came to talk to you about a job."

"Mr. Wagner—"

"Leland, dear. You're part of the family now."

"Leland," she almost choked on the name, feeling like a fraud. "I really don't want to use Donovan's position to garner business. It really feels too much like nepotism. I'd prefer making it on my own. I hope you understand."

There. That was clear and to the point. No handouts for Sarah Madison, thank you very much.

"Hasn't Donovan told you that I never do anything to be nice?" Leland asked.

Despite herself, Sarah chuckled. "He hasn't, but even if he did, I wouldn't believe him."

"Well, that's insulting," the older man said with a humph for emphasis. "Do you think I'm losing some of my meanness just because I'm no longer taking court cases?"

"Sir—"

"Leland."

"Leland, I don't believe you ever had any meanness."

The older man sighed and tried to look insulted, but there was a twinkle in his hazel eyes that told Sarah he wasn't a bit.

"Well, just to put your fears to rest," he said, "I'll tell you that since Donovan introduced you, I've done some checking on my own. I've seen the work you did for Ratgaz."

"How did you manage that?"

"Donovan had pictures taken to use as evidence for your case. And let me tell you that my approaching you with a job has nothing at all to do with nepotism, but rather it has to do with me wanting the best. That's why I hired Donovan to work for the firm, and that's why I'm here.''

"You just saw one office," she felt compelled to point out. "And just pictures of it to boot.''

"One office complex. You did the whole floor. It was enough. I know you're good at what you do. The reception area at the office needs to be addressed, and I believe in the best for my firm, whether it's hiring associates, or decorators. I'm approaching you on your own merits, not on some connection through Donovan.''

"But—''

"Are you telling me you don't want the business?'' Leland asked, a white, bushy eyebrow rising.

Sarah sighed. She didn't just want the business, she needed it. "No, I'm not telling you I don't want it.''

"Are you telling me you're not good?''

She sat up straight in her chair. "I'm the best.''

"Well then, I'm at the right place. Now, Donovan mentioned you had some ideas already?''

"They were just off the top of my head," she said.

"Why don't you tell me what you were thinking, and if I agree, you can work up a more formal plan and we'll discuss fees.''

Sarah found herself becoming more and more excited about her plans for the reception area. And as she and Leland discussed her ideas and his needs, she almost forgot the mess she'd made of her life.

By the time Donovan's senior partner left, Sarah was so wrapped up in her ideas for his reception area, that she'd totally forgotten her predicament. She'd moved back into her private office and was busily trying to capture her initial ideas, when the buzzer sounded again.

She'd forgotten to lock the door when Leland left. That just went to show how distracted she was. She never forgot to lock up.

Before she could move, Donovan walked in and, without preamble, said, "How long will it take you to pack?"

Sarah dropped her sketch pad and stood. "What do you mean?"

"I mean, we should have discussed this yesterday at breakfast, but I'll admit, when you said yes you'd marry me, I was so unprepared, that I sort of lost my focus. And afterward, I thought a night to let things sink in, to let you adjust, was probably wise."

What Donovan didn't add was he wasn't accustomed to losing his focus...ever. He wasn't sure he liked it. As a matter of fact, he was sure he didn't like it at all.

"But you can't keep living here," he continued, a little harsher than he'd intended to, "so you're coming home with me."

"I won't live with you before we're married." Her lips pressed together in a stubborn line.

Donovan was suddenly hit with the urge to kiss the tightness away.

Kiss Sarah?

No, that wouldn't do. This was business, not pleasure. He had to remember that.

"Sarah, be rational. Since we're not sharing a bedroom, even after we're married, it doesn't matter when you move in. It's not as if I'm planning to ravish you."

He wasn't planning to, but that didn't stop him from fantasizing about it. Ravishing Sarah was something he hadn't completely been able to put out of his mind. During the daytime, he was able to relegate the thought to the recesses of his awareness, but at night...

His dreams about her had nothing to do with a platonic business arrangement, and everything to do with her belonging to him completely, in a more binding way than any contractual bargain could forge.

But that didn't make sense.

He could scarcely spare the time this arrangement was already costing him. He certainly couldn't spare time for anything more distracting.

"Listen," he said more gruffly than he'd intended, "I have work to do and I don't have time to argue. Pack your things, and move into my guest room now."

"No."

Now Sarah's lips weren't just stubborn-looking. No, she'd set her hands on her hips and looked ready to fight him.

"It will simply strengthen the idea of a serious relationship in people's minds," he said.

"No."

"I insist." There was no accidental gruffness this time. Oh, no. It was totally intentional. Couldn't she see that living here was ridiculous? This was a two-room building, with a closet-size bathroom that didn't even have a shower or a tub. She slept on a sleeper-sofa. His place would be safer and more comfortable.

Obviously she wasn't so easy to convince because her hands were still on her hips as she shook her head and said, "Listen, you can insist all you want to your colleagues, your clients, or the court. But your insisting means nothing to me."

"Please?"

Where did that come from? *Please?* Donovan wasn't the type of man who *asked*—he *told*. And yet, asking Sarah to do something for him seemed to be becoming a habit. He'd asked her to play his fiancée, asked her to marry him, and now he was asking her to move in. He wasn't sure he liked this trend.

Obviously Sarah was as surprised to hear him asking as he was, because she asked, "What did you say?" as if she thought she must be hearing things.

"Please," he repeated. The word didn't even catch

in his throat. "If insisting doesn't work, I thought asking might. I can't stand having you live like this. I dropped you off yesterday and went home to work on the Dawson brief. Only I couldn't. This place doesn't have any security…that's something else we need to discuss, even if you're not living here, a good security system."

"It's got locks, that's secure enough."

He sighed. She was going to be difficult. That was another great reason for waiting to get married…women were inherently difficult, and reasoning with them took way too long.

"Listen, it's after hours, and I just walked right in. You hadn't even locked the front door."

"I normally do, only I got so caught up in some sketches, that I forgot. I won't let it happen again, if that will make you feel better."

"It won't," he assured her.

"Well, I'm sorry Donovan, but I'm not moving."

"Fine." He tossed his briefcase into the corner and made himself at home on the couch. "What time do we go to the Y tomorrow?"

"What?"

"For a shower. What time do you get up to go to the Y? And do you order dinner in, or go out? It's obvious you do one or the other, since there's no kitchen here. And I'm hungry, so whichever way you handle things, could we get dinner now? I can't think on an empty stomach, and I have to finish this brief tonight.''

''What are you talking about?''

''If you won't move in with me, I guess I'm moving in here until the wedding. Although—'' he looked down at the couch ''—I think the two of us on this sleeper-sofa might get a bit cramped. But whatever makes you comfortable and keeps you safe.''

''You think you're moving in here?'' Sarah asked. She appeared to be trying to decide if she should laugh, or be annoyed.

''Yes.'' He eyed the small wardrobe. ''And do you think you can clear out half of that, so I can hang up a few suits?''

Annoyance must have won out because he couldn't miss the emotion in her voice as she said, ''You're insane. You're not moving in here. This office is cramped enough with just me.''

''Ah, then you've decided to move into my place? Great. Let's go. I'll cook you something for dinner.''

''No. That's not what I meant. I meant, you're going to your house, and I'm staying here.''

''Sorry. That wasn't one of the options. You're staying with me, in my nice, big, comfortable, shower-equipped house, or I'm staying here in your small, cramped, showerless office.''

''This isn't a negotiation. I agreed to help you out—and have been wondering all day why—but I didn't agree to your stepping in and trying to take over my life. Forget it, the deal's off."

"Fine, I'll see you in court then," he said, standing.

"You're still going to take care of Ratgaz?" She offered a small smile, "Thank you, Donovan."

"There's that. After all, our initial deal was, you be my fiancée for a night, I sue Ratgaz. You did that, so Ratgaz will pay, I guarantee you. But I'll also see you in court because I'm suing you. Breach of contract."

"Suing me?" She laughed for a moment, but then she looked at him and he saw the dawning of understanding in her face as she protested. "I didn't sign anything."

"Ah, but you made an oral contract with me. You said you'd marry me."

"I changed my mind."

"No. You're simply mad that negotiations aren't going your way. That's not a good enough reason to break a contract."

"You're insane."

"And you're beautiful." Did he say that out loud? Hurrying, he covered by saying, "But we still have an oral contract, and neither of those points directly affects it. Now, the question remains—my place, or yours?"

"I—"

"Sarah, you don't have to live like this. I shouldn't

have come in here and just told you to pack, I should have discussed it with you. I'm not the kind of man who's used to asking. I'm sorry. There. I'm not used to apologizing either, but I have.''

He paused, trying to think how to reach her and make her see his plan was best for both of them. ''It's just that I won't get any work done worrying about you here. Last night showed me that. I'm simply asking you to stay with me, in my guest room. Nothing ominous. Nothing to compromise our agreement. I just want you safe.''

''Donovan, you're taking this engagement thing far too seriously. It's just business. You don't owe me anything, and even if you did, I can take care of myself.''

''Maybe. But I'd worry if any of my colleagues at the firm were living like this.''

''It's not so bad.'' She shrugged her shoulders. ''Really.''

He wondered who she was trying to convince, him or herself?

''You're seriously going to tell me you'd rather rough it here than stay at my place where you've got little things like kitchens and showers?'' he asked gently.

She sighed as she said, ''No.''

''Then say yes, you'll stay with me. At least give it a try.''

''I guess it wouldn't hurt to try.''

"You're going to be living there after the wedding anyway."

"There is that."

Before she could change her mind and think up any other arguments, he said, "So go pack."

Sarah had jumped from the frying pan into the fire. Of course, it was a rather nice fire…that had burned under some wonderful steaks on the grill. The tantalizing odor still lingered, even as Sarah finished her last bite of the tender meat and took a sip of a nice non-screw-on-cap wine Donovan had poured her.

She was going to get spoiled, living like this. It wasn't just the wine, or having someone cook for her. No, what she envied most about Donovan's place was this view. Sitting on the deck, looking out over Erie's bay. Sailboats puffed by. Powerboats occasionally rumbled past.

She could see Presque Isle peninsula across the bay, and the occasional reflection off a car driving its length.

Yes, she liked the view. It was marvelous. Even in the winter, when the bay would be frozen over, she'd be able to enjoy it from the warmth of Donovan's kitchen and its wall of glass.

"What are you thinking?" Donovan asked, breaking the silence.

"That I love looking at the water."

"Me, too. I wasn't planning on buying a condo. I

wanted a house. But when the real-estate agent insisted on showing me this, I signed the papers right away because of this view.''

''I don't blame you. Maybe you should add something to the prenup that I get visitation rights after we're divorced. Say dinner, once a month just so I can enjoy the deck?''

''You've got it.'' He grinned.

Sarah breathed a sigh of relief. Things seemed easier than she'd anticipated. Maybe, just maybe, this would work out all right.

Sarah said, ''You're right, you know.''

''I know. But I'm right about so many things, what specific thing am I right about this time?''

''If this is an example of your cooking ability, you get to keep that particular job. Make a note for the prenup, would you?''

''Sarah gets visitation rights for my deck, and I get to cook for the length of our marriage. Anything else?''

''I'm sure I'll think of something.''

''I don't doubt that in the least. I've been thinking about the prenup—''

Whatever Donovan had been thinking and was going to say was cut short by the doorbell.

''Were you expecting someone?'' Sarah asked. ''I could go unpack.''

She felt uncomfortable being caught here in his home. Almost guilty. It wasn't as if she had anything to be guilty about. This was a platonic business arrangement. She wasn't shacking up with someone and living in sin.

Maybe that was the source of her guilt. Sitting across the table, looking out at the bay and sipping wine, she could almost forget that this was business, and begin to think it was something more.

The idea of *something more* with Donovan might appeal to her if she weren't wrapped up in this absurd charade. As a matter of fact, her sleep had been punctuated with dreams of Donovan ever since he'd slipped his ring on her finger.

Dreams of the two of them and *something more*.

"See, this living together is going to cramp your style," she said.

"I have no style, and no, I'm not expecting anyone. I'll be right back. Just finish your dinner. You left some baked potato. Clean the plate. You don't eat enough."

"With the way you feed me, I'm going to be waddling before this marriage is over," Sarah grumbled to herself.

Donovan seemed obsessed with feeding her, she thought after he disappeared. And yet—she speared the last bite of potato from her plate—he did manage to feed her such wonderful things. She pushed the plate back and stared at a sailboat zigzagging through the water.

"Oh, Sarah, we got so much done today," a decidedly female voice said.

Sarah turned and saw Mrs. Wagner and Donovan in the doorway. "Come into the living room, dear. The girls are setting things up." Mrs. Wagner turned and bustled back through the sliding glass doors.

"How did they find me here?" Sarah whispered.

He looked guilty, and said, "I might have mentioned to Leland that you were moving in."

"So now everyone knows I'm living with you?" The very thought made her uncomfortable.

Donovan shrugged. He didn't look the least bit concerned as he answered. "Like I said, it makes us look more like a couple."

A couple of fools, that's what they were. Thinking this marriage could work out. Sarah stalked into the living room and forced herself to smile as she looked at the women's excited faces.

"Oh, Sarah, sit down, dear," Mrs. Wagner said. "Just wait until you see what we've accomplished today."

"I have a tent reserved. We don't want rain ruining your day. And they have heaters, too. Just in case it's cold," Brigitta said.

"We are living in Erie, after all. Even July can get a cold front." Hanni laughed and so did everyone else.

The standing joke in town was that if you didn't

like the weather in Erie you just had to wait a few minutes for it to change.

Mrs. Wagner patted the cushion next to her. "Sit down, dear. We can be overwhelming, but I promise we won't bite."

"Speak for three out of four of us. Remember that time Brigitta bit me when we were…oh, I don't know, seven and eight? She left a scar." Liesl pointed to a spot on her arm.

Sarah didn't see anything, but she nodded as she took her seat next to Mrs. Wagner.

"That's okay, you cut my hair, remember?" Brigitta said.

"As you can see, raising the girls was sometimes more like being a lion trainer than a mom," Mrs. Wagner said with a laugh. "Now, I talked to Leland's friend, Mathias—"

"That's Judge Long, for those who didn't grow up in the courthouse," Liesl said, interrupting.

Her mother shot her a warning look and continued, "—and he'd be honored to perform the ceremony. Donovan knows him."

"So now the big question is…dresses," said Hanni.

"Dresses?" Sarah had just barely started to adjust to the idea of marrying Donovan, but she hadn't really thought about what a wedding would entail. Dresses, tents, judges…and probably flowers, and food.

Oh, God, what had she done? She didn't want all

this. If she was going to go through with this sham of a marriage, maybe she could talk Donovan into just eloping somewhere.

But one look at the four women's excited faces, and she knew she couldn't do that. They were all so delighted.

"Dresses," she said with a sigh. "I hadn't thought about them."

"You haven't thought about much," Liesl said. "That's because this is all moving so fast."

"But we love Donovan, despite the fact he's not teddy-bear cuddly. He puts on a tough front, but underneath we always suspected there was a warm mushy side, and it's more evident with you around. We just can't see the two of you waiting a year for the wedding of your dreams," Brigitta said.

"Yeah, if I weren't married," Hanni added, her voice soft and conspiratorial, "I'd snap him up for myself and see if I could thaw The Iceman."

"But you are," her mother reminded her. "Don't make Sarah nervous. We've never seen Donovan look at anyone the way he looked at you Friday night. That's why we don't want you two to wait. Now, about the dresses."

"For you and the bridesmaids," Liesl clarified.

"Donovan can take care of tuxes," Hanni said.

"How many?" Brigitta asked.

Sarah felt as if she'd been sucked down the rabbit hole with Alice. "How many what?" she asked.

"Bridesmaids. How many do you think you want?" Mrs. Wagner said.

"I hadn't thought about it, about any of it other than to think a fall wedding would be lovely."

"And it will be," Mrs. Wagner soothed. "I went to a wedding once with eight bridesmaids, but I thought that was overkill. I had three."

"I only had one," Hanni said. "That's all you really need. Just someone to witness the wedding for you."

"One," Sarah said, shooting Hanni a grateful look. "I guess just one. I don't have a big extended family, and I'm an only child. So there are no feelings to hurt."

"Small and elegant. Oh, you have such good taste," Liesl said.

"Here." Brigitta plopped a stack of magazines on Sarah's lap. "Let's see what you're leaning toward. Maybe this weekend we could actually go try some on."

"Now, who's your bridesmaid going to be?"

Chapter Seven

Donovan hid in the kitchen, doing the dishes—that was his excuse if anyone asked. Although no one had. Doing dishes was a good excuse though. Avoiding the women was the real reason. He figured traditionally the groom just had to show up at the wedding, and that worked for him.

He was a traditional sort of guy.

But as much as he didn't want to plan the wedding, he couldn't help sneaking a look at the women from time to time.

Mrs. Wagner, Hanni, Liesl and Brigitta, surrounded Sarah. They bombarded her with plans. And at first Sarah seemed ill at ease, but as they studied wedding gowns in the magazines, she seemed to relax and started to enjoy herself.

Bits of the conversation made their way into the kitchen.

"...No, no, dear. You want something to emphasize your beautiful hair. Not a full veil," Mrs. Wagner scolded.

"It's red. I always thought I looked like a giant red Popsicle. Tall, skinny and red. Yuck."

"Are you crazy? Not skinny, slender. And tall is good, especially next to Donovan's height. And your hair is gorgeous..."

It was, Donovan reflected.

There was such a mix of colors in her hair. Red, of course, but there were streaks of lighter, almost blond, strands. And the small curls seemed to take on a life of their own, on occasion. There was one curl that had escaped Sarah's barrette and wrapped itself around her left ear at dinner. It drove him nuts. He wanted to reach over and tuck it in. And conversely, he wanted to reach over and pull out the barrette and let the rest of her curls free.

He'd dreamed about her hair...about her. Sarah, leaning over him, those red curls spilling down and tickling his face. He'd reached up to touch them, to pull her to him...and woke up to find his hands full of a pillow.

He'd tossed the thing across the room and spent the rest of the night wide awake and restless. That's when he started to worry about Sarah, alone in a building with no security. Sleeping on a couch. A bathroom with no shower.

By the time the sun had crept over the horizon, he had himself worked up into quite a state. It was easier to blame Sarah's living arrangement than his dreams.

He'd just put the last plate away when Mrs. Wagner called, "Donovan, come out here, would you?"

His living room was a blizzard of papers and magazines. Remembering Sarah's comments about his messy office, he wondered how she was dealing with his now messy living room. A mess that was entirely her fault.

He smiled at the thought. "Yes, Mrs. Wagner?"

"This is your wedding, too, and we're trying to convince Sarah that we should go all out. She keeps trying to rein us in."

"I just want to keep things small," Sarah said. "I don't want a huge ceremony. Just something small and tasteful with a few friends."

"And family," Brigitta added.

"And family," Sarah parroted back.

Though she was smiling, Donovan could detect the lack of enthusiasm in her expression. He could read her with surprising ease. She was thinking of expense and worrying about the less than romantic aspect of their nuptials.

"So what do you think, Donovan?" Mrs. Wagner asked.

"I think that whatever Sarah wants is fine with me."

"I just can't see spending all kinds of money on—" Sarah stopped short.

She was going to bring up the whole business-relationship thing—would have if they weren't surrounded by some of the very people who couldn't know the real nature of their relationship.

Donovan quickly filled in, "On something that is a private, solemn ceremony. Two people joining their lives and their hopes. Two people sharing their dreams and working to see them come true. Two people agreeing to take life as it comes…together," he supplied. "You're right, Sarah. Something small and special is just what I want to commemorate that type of agreement."

He turned to Mrs. Wagner and her daughters. "That's why your hosting the wedding at your home is so wonderful. It just adds to the intimacy of the day."

"Why, Donovan," Mrs. Wagner said with a small sniff, "I didn't realize how…well, poetic you could be, dear."

"I didn't either, at least not until Sarah came into my life."

"Oh, Sarah, you've done wonders for our Donovan. Leland was simply worrying himself to death over the boy's ambitions. He, Leland, not Donovan, always says that ambition is all well and good, but family…that's what makes life worth living. When the girls were young, he was still working to establish his career and the firm, but no matter what he had going on, the girls came first. At the beginning of each month, he'd pull out his planner and write down all their important events. Basketball games, track meets, open houses, various ceremonies. He bent over backwards to get to all of them."

"I can't think of anything important Dad ever missed," Hanni said. "He was always there. Most nights he was home in time to read to us before bed when we were small."

"When we got older," Liesl agreed, "he'd come in and listen to all three of us try to tell him about our days at once."

"That's what he wants for you Donovan," Mrs. Wagner said, her voice soft. "He says he thinks you're such a talented attorney. He just wants you to take some of that talent and drive, and funnel it into something that will matter long after practicing the law is a memory. Family. He's so pleased that you've found out what matters."

Donovan didn't know what to say, so he said nothing.

Silence. That was comfortable and familiar. This? All this talk about emotions and family…he didn't quite know what to do with it.

He'd never quite figured out what led him to accept a position at Wagner, McDuffy and Chambers. It wasn't the job he'd always dreamed of, and yet, when the offers started rolling in, it was the one that felt right. And though he wasn't a man who usually made decisions based on feelings rather than facts, he'd done just that and accepted the position with Leland Wagner.

Sarah reached over and squeezed his hand, and said, "I have no doubts that Donovan is the best attorney at the firm, and he's already given me so much that I think you can assure Mr. Wagner that he knows what's important. Now, about the flowers, I was thinking we could just pick up some inexpensive mums. It will keep with the fall theme and…"

He realized that Sarah was still holding his hand as she led the women into a new conversational direction. He gave it a quick squeeze of thanks and didn't let go as he tried to process the impact of his conversation with Mrs. Wagner.

When they'd had the meeting about partnership, Leland had said the same thing…balance. He wanted that for Donovan. And balance is what Donovan feared he'd never have. That's why he'd put off having a family. He wanted to make sure he was at a point in his career that he could find time for them.

But would that time ever come?

Once he made partner and established himself in the position, would he cut back enough on his practice to build a relationship, or would he continue to steam forward, always looking for more acclaim, more power, more money? What was enough?

Would there ever be time for the type of relationship he wanted? A relationship like Leland had with his wife?

Donovan didn't know. What he did know was that he didn't want the type of relationship his parents had. Family was secondary to business. Whenever something happened at school, it had been his grandmother who'd been there. Most of his friends never met his parents.

He fingered the ring—his grandmother's ring—on Sarah's finger. He wanted...

He wanted what Leland and Mrs. Wagner had. What his grandmother had had with his grandfather.

But the way he was going he'd never have it. He'd have power, he'd have a practice other lawyers envied, but he'd never have this...a room full of people laughing and talking. He couldn't remember the last time he'd had someone to his place before Sarah.

He studied her. She'd had his attention long before this fake engagement. What was it about her that was different than all the other women he'd known?

"You're awful quiet, Donovan," Mrs. Wagner said.

"Just thinking."

"About what? Oh, don't answer that. I could see the way you were looking at Sarah and I can imagine what you were thinking," she said with a laugh. "Believe it or not, Leland and I were young once, too."

"I've seen how Dad looks at you, Mom, and I have no doubts that age isn't what matters, feelings are. That's what all of us wanted in a relationship, what you and Dad have. That's what we insisted on. And it looks like that's what Donovan wanted as well," Liesl said.

"Oh, there's the door," Hanni announced. "I invited Amelia over, and I think she said there were a few other ladies who were coming with her."

The door opened and there was a wave of women crashing into Donovan's quiet home.

"I think it's time for me to let you ladies go at it," Donovan said, standing, and letting go of Sarah's hand as he did so.

"We've got pizza," Amelia called as she rushed into the room, pizza boxes in her hand followed by a swarm of other women.

"Nice digs, Donovan," Pearly said. "It took Sarah to get us here. Ah, but that's what women are for…to force a man into sociability. Why, did I ever tell you all about my Uncle Turtle? He spent three years living on his own in a tiny cabin middle of nowhere. Then—"

Josie, Snips And Snaps's big-haired, bubble-gum-blowing manicurist, interrupted Pearly. "Now, don't you start on another one of your stories. We're here to plan a wedding not to talk about some recluse uncle—''

''—Uncle Turtle was only a recluse until—''

''Oh, hush,'' Mabel, Perry Square's acupuncturist, scolded. ''Now, Sarah, darling, Libby said you just plan on everyone getting their hair done at Snips And Snaps before the wedding. She'll be here as soon as she gets Meg tucked in for the night.''

''Oh, honey,'' Josie said, finding a space on the floor next to the coffee table that was now loaded with pizza, ''I have this great new polish called Bride's Blush we'll do your nails with and...''

''Have fun,'' Donovan called as he walked out of his living room and back toward the quieter clime of his office, sure that he'd never be missed.

''Coward,'' Sarah called.

He turned and gave her a small nod, admitting his cowardice. He could face a judge and a jury, but there was no way he could face a room full of women with weddings on their minds.

Sarah laughed at his silent admission, and the sight of her surrounded by people in his living room laughing caused some strange constriction in Donovan's chest.

Something he didn't quite understand and wasn't sure he wanted to.

Sarah wasn't laughing two hours later when the place was quiet. She picked up pizza boxes, stacked magazines, and wondered how on earth she'd ended up here.

While everyone was talking and planning, she'd fallen into the spirit of things and forgotten the true nature of her situation.

She was engaged to be married, living with a man and planning a wedding. A man she hardly knew and didn't love. Oh, maybe she lusted over him, at least a little.

That first time she'd met him, when he'd burst into her office as she tried to unpack…oh, how she'd lusted. He'd been dripping wet and his monosyllabic responses hadn't been enough to dim the immediate rush of desire that swept through her body, leaving her feeling a bit breathless and weak in the knees.

But desire wasn't any more satisfying a reason to marry than business was.

How had she gotten here? she asked herself for what seemed like the hundredth time.

"Are they gone?" Donovan stage-whispered as he walked into the room.

"Coward," she repeated.

"No. Simply wise."

"You deserted me."

"You seemed to be enjoying yourself," he said, helping her by picking up the pizza boxes.

"I did. At least part of the time. Then I'd remember that this was all pretend and…"

"I wish you'd stop that."

The annoyance in his voice caused her to snap her focus onto him. "What?"

"Worrying about clarifying exactly what our relationship is. It's whatever we make it. Whatever we want it to be. Maybe it started in an unconventional manner—at least unconventional by today's standards—but it's a valid and meaningful relationship."

"Valid as a means of attaining a partnership."

"It's whatever we make it," he said again.

"Are you going to put that into the prenup? *This relationship is whatever we make it?* You can add it to our growing list. Let's see, you cook, you pay for everything—"

"Hey, you're buying groceries," he pointed out.

"And I get visitation with the deck. And I'm redecorating your office, as well as a few other potential jobs." She paused. "Somehow it seems I'm coming out way ahead on this deal. There must be something else you want."

"Now that you mention it, there is." His voice had a new quality to it, softer and richer.

Sarah felt a little unnerved. "What? Just pull out that trusty legal pad you've been scribbling notes on and write it down. What is it you want out of all this, Donovan?"

"I'm getting a partnership," he said.

There was more. She wasn't sure what it was, but he was trying to hide it. "That's old. That's already part of the deal. What else?"

"This." He stepped forward, so close she could feel the heat radiating from his body.

Sarah wasn't sure what she expected. Maybe something along the lines of a demand that she wash his car once a week, or she do the laundry. Yeah, washing clothes was definitely more in line with what she was thinking.

Instead, his lips drew closer, as if in slow motion, and she knew just what he wanted. She could pull away. She knew he'd let her. But instead, she moved forward and her lips met his.

Nothing else touched except their lips, leaving Sarah an open window of escape if she chose it. But she didn't.

She welcomed this kiss. It was a soft introduction…hardly more than a peck.

Donovan pulled back, breaking the short contact, and stood there looking at her as if she had suddenly grown a second nose.

Sarah ran a finger lightly over her lips just to make sure they were unchanged. "What do you call that?"

"A kiss?" he said, a questioning tone still in his voice.

"No," she argued. She focused on Donovan's lips. They were perfectly ordinary lips. A tannish pink. Not too full or too thin. They were nice enough, she guessed. But that didn't explain the earthshaking feeling she'd had when they'd touched hers. But she wasn't going to call it a kiss. A kiss implied…well, more than she was willing to infer from the contact.

"Your lips barely touched mine. It was just a light graze. Why, if it hadn't been our lips, but our elbows—"

"Elbows?" he asked.

Elbows.

She forced her gaze from Donovan's lips to his elbows. They were nice, but didn't make her knees shake like his lips did.

"Yes," she said. "If our elbows had touched that briefly, that softly, why we'd never have noticed it."

"I'd have noticed," he assured her.

"No you wouldn't. You'd have simply kept walking right by me, if our elbows had accidentally grazed."

"But it wasn't our elbows, it was our lips, and it wasn't an accident."

"It wasn't?" she asked, though she knew it wasn't. She'd seen his intent and welcomed it.

"No," he said. "I've been wanting to do that for a long time."

"Why?" Sarah asked. In all the reasons he'd argued for a marriage, kissing was never one of them.

"Why what?" he asked.

"Why would you…"

"Kiss you?" he filled in helpfully.

"No. Graze. Why would your lips graze mine *on purpose*. This is a farce and we're business partners.

Do your lips frequently graze your law-practice partner's on purpose?''

"Ah, but I'm not a partner yet, just an associate," he pointed out.

Was he joking again? Sarah decided then and there she didn't like a joking Donovan any more than she liked a grazing one. "But when you're a partner, and not just an associate, will you be planning on more grazing then?''

"You make us sound like a herd of cows," he said.

"You're avoiding my question."

"What was your question?''

"Why did you..." She didn't want to say graze again. He was right, it did sound as if she was talking about cows, so she settled for, "Why did you peck me on the lips on purpose.''

"Ah, pecking. So we're not cows, but chickens?'' he asked.

"We're no farmyard animal. And we're not doing that again.''

"You didn't like it?'' he asked.

"No." Okay, that was a lie, but Sarah wasn't about to admonish herself for it. She wasn't going to take it back either. Better he think she didn't enjoy what they'd just done.

"Well, why didn't you like it?'' he asked, sounding put out.

"I don't want your lips touching mine on purpose again.'' She took a full step backward.

There. She'd put enough space between them. He couldn't reach her to kiss her on purpose again. She'd just have to be sure to maintain a nonpecking distance from him in the future.

"How about if my lips touch yours by accident?"

Just to be safe, she took another step backward so his lips couldn't touch hers accidentally either.... "No. You keep your lips off this partner, unless you're going to go around kissing your other partners, too."

"Associates. We're just associates for now."

"Whatever. No more."

"Why are you so upset?" he asked, taking a step toward her.

"Because I am." She eyed the space separating them and decided she needed more than space, she needed a door. She hurried toward her room. "Listen, I'm going to bed now."

"Do you need a bedtime story?" he called. The proximity of his voice suggested he hadn't stayed put.

She turned and saw he was a couple steps behind her. "No."

"Then I don't suppose you want to be tucked in either, right?"

"Right."

"Because if I tucked you in, I'd have to kiss you good-night," he pointed out.

"Good night," she cried, because she wasn't sure what else to say. The image of Donovan leaning over and kissing her good-night was too intense for any more logical arguments to get around.

She stepped into her room and called, "Good night," again.

"Sweet dreams," he whispered. He'd followed her and was close enough to whisper, his voice all husky and inviting. The kind of voice she'd love to have tell her a bedtime story...one that involved lips.

Sarah sighed as she shut her bedroom door, leaving him on the other side of it in the hall. She knew the truth of things. There would be no sweet dreams tonight or any night in her near future. Not as long as she was living in this nightmare.

Why on earth had he kissed Sarah and then picked on her like that?

Okay, that was a two-part question, Donovan told himself as he stood on the deck watching the lights bob across the bay.

Part one—why did he kiss her?

Because he'd been dying to for such a long time. Since that day he'd stumbled into her shop, if he was honest with himself. At that very moment, looking at her surprised face, he'd wanted to pull her into his arms and kiss her.

And watching her all summer in the park, eating her lunch by herself, sketching, or occasionally sitting with Amelia, chatting and laughing. Well, he had fantasized about kissing her all those times. And that was before he'd known her. She'd been just a face. A lovely face, but just a shell.

Now he knew that what was inside was more beautiful than what was outside, and that made her even more tempting. More kissable.

Now he'd done it.

He hadn't planned on it, hadn't set out to let it happen. And he wasn't going to reflect on whether or not that one kiss was enough. No, he was going to ignore the fact that he wasn't satisfied and could easily go wake her up and kiss her again.

Part two—why had he behaved so poorly? He could have simply apologized. Blamed the kiss on too much wine or the excitement of planning a wedding.

Instead he'd hounded her, picked on her like some second grader tying a girl's pigtails together.

That was definitely not a characteristic he generally employed. But then again, marrying a woman he was sexually attracted to was out of the norm for him as well.

Nothing had been normal since Sarah had come into his life. All he was left with was a question...was he better off now, or before?

Donovan thought he knew the answer and wasn't sure he liked it.

Chapter Eight

"Mrs. Lewis, how are you today?" Donovan asked the gray-haired lady who bustled into his office without knocking. She carried a brown grocery bag in one hand, a cane in the other.

He knew from experience that she wouldn't ask how he was, which was good because he wouldn't have known how to answer. Three weeks had passed since he'd kissed Sarah, and though he could think of little else, they hadn't repeated it.

"How am I? How am I, he asks," Mrs. Lewis said. "Not good. Not good at all, Donovan."

Donovan wasn't sure who she was talking to when she started since they were the only two people in the office, but since she answered herself, he pretty much figured it was a rhetorical question.

The more-than-middle-aged woman—she'd have sued Donovan in a heartbeat if he even thought the word *old*—opened the bag and started pulling out bowls and plates.

"Problems?" he asked.

"I've decided not to cut Stuart out of the will. You were right. He's an idiot, but he's not mean-spirited. And since being an idiot was pretty much a given considering who his parents were, I can't hold that against him."

"Well, I'm sure he'd be pleased to hear you think so."

Mrs. Lewis had built a healthy little nest egg and visited every Wednesday at lunch to discuss changing her will. She never did. Donovan thought of their Wednesday lunches as Mrs. Lewis's therapy sessions. She vented, he listened and ate. And when she was in a particularly good mood, he sometimes conned her out of recipes.

She was a wonderful cook.

"But I'm thinking my niece Sally is out."

Donovan reached over and scribbled Sally on a legal pad. He was willing to let Mrs. Lewis distract him from his own problems. "Okay, Sally's out of the will. May I ask why?"

Mrs. Lewis handed him a plate as she started. "Well, rumor has it she thinks I'm controlling. Me? Controlling? I can't imagine where she got that idea. Why just last week…"

Donovan listened, nodding at the appropriate times, as he took his first bite of the crab salad Mrs. Lewis had handed him.

"Ma'am, I'm not belittling or ignoring your complaints about Sally, but I have to interrupt you to say that this is the best crab salad I've ever tasted."

She stopped and beamed. "Oh, I just knew you'd like it. I had to dig the recipe out. Haven't made it since Herbert's last birthday. It was always his favorite. You want to know the secret?"

Secret.

Donovan wished he knew the secret of what was going on between him and Sarah. If he didn't know better, he'd think—

"Donovan, are you listening, boy? I asked if you wanted to know the secret recipe."

"Sorry. I drifted a minute. And you know I want any recipe I can get you to share."

"Dill. Just a tiny bit of dill in the dressing really brings all the flavors together."

"Do I get the whole thing?" he asked with just the proper amount of pleading in his voice.

Mrs. Lewis beamed. "It just so happens I wrote it down for you. I never met a man who liked to cook as much as you do. You'll make some woman a dandy wife someday." She chortled at her own joke.

"It just so happens, I've already got the woman lined up."

Now why on earth had he said that? Other than the

office, he hadn't told anyone about his wedding. Which reminded him, he'd have to call his parents. Invitations were going out this week.

Damn. He didn't want to go into this with them.

How could he explain his marriage to Sarah to his parents when he didn't understand it himself? He should be thrilled. After all, he was getting the marriage he needed with no expectations on her part. He was marrying a woman he couldn't hurt, because you couldn't hurt someone who didn't love you.

Rather than relief at the thought, Donovan felt more restless, almost annoyed, though he didn't know why.

"Why, you sly dog," Mrs. Lewis exclaimed. "You let me come in here every week and all this time you've got news like that? Who is she?"

"You know the new shop on the square, By Design? The owner. Sarah Madison. Soon to be Sarah Madison-Donovan."

Saying the new configuration of her name made him wonder if she'd use Donovan at all. She'd probably keep using Madison. After all, it made sense. That way she wouldn't have to change everything back when the marriage ended.

The thought left him feeling more out-of-sorts.

He forced himself not to worry about last names and continued what he'd started. "We're going to be married in just a few weeks. Small, and informal, but I was hoping you'd come."

"Are you inviting me in hopes of making it into my will?" Mrs. Lewis asked, laughing.

He tried to give her the stern look he knew she expected, but couldn't help but smile. "That would be unethical, and I think you know better. Besides, if I was in it, we both know I'd be out of it before you ever got a signature on it."

At that Mrs. Lewis clapped her hands. "Oh, you think you know me so well."

"I think perhaps I do." Despite her money, Mrs. Lewis was a lonely lady.

"So sure of yourself," she said.

"No, so sure of you."

"So what do you think you know?" she asked, leaning closer to the desk.

"That despite the way you talk about your family, you love them all desperately."

"So why do I come in here every week to change my will if I love them all so much?"

"Because it just so happens you like me, too." He grinned and folded his arms across his chest at the proclamation.

Theirs was an odd friendship, but he'd learned a lot from Mrs. Lewis.

"Does this fiancée know she's getting a man with a swelled head and there's a risk he won't be able to fit through the chapel doors?"

"Maybe that's why she's planned an outdoor wedding."

"Now, that's something I have to see. So where's my invitation?" she demanded.

"In the mail, or it will be soon."

"Humph. It better be. Because when I was looking for this crab salad recipe, I happened to come across a cake...chocolate and strawberries, and this creme filling that's to die for. Just the thing to woo a new wife. I think I'll just hold that recipe hostage until my invitation comes."

"You're a sly woman, Mrs. Lewis. I'll have to hurry and address one and get it out."

"See that you do," she said with a humph that was completely all show.

"About cutting Sally out of the will?" he asked.

"You just draw up the papers and I'll see how I feel next week when I come in." She started clearing the lunch things. "And I'd better have my invitation by then as well."

"I'll see to it that you do."

The old woman did something totally uncharacteristic...she walked around the desk and kissed Donovan on the cheek. "You be happy, boy. As happy as Mr. Lewis and I were. Remember, if you love someone you can work through any of the tough times. You can do anything...if you love each other."

"Thanks, Mrs. Lewis."

Donovan watched her go.

If you loved someone.

The sentence rattled around in his head.

But love wasn't a factor in his relationship with Sarah. Granted, the last three weeks had been some of the best he could remember.

They'd established a routine. He still cooked, but she was his self-appointed assistant. They came home, poured a couple glasses of wine and made dinner together. It was a small thing. Nothing big. They prepared dinner and talked of their days.

He listened to her talk with enthusiasm about her new projects. She listened to him talk about his cases. They continued talking as they ate, and then cleaned up.

Then they sat in the living room and did work, or watched a television show.

Small things.

And every night he walked down the hall with her. They both said a chaste good-night outside their doors and went to their own respective bedrooms.

The walls weren't thick enough to keep Donovan from hearing her getting ready for bed. They weren't thick enough to keep him from being aware of her presence.

Brick wouldn't have been thick enough for that.

And every night he went to bed and dreamed...of Sarah. Of the little things. In his dreams there was no worry about the temporary nature of their wedding, no worry about careers. There was just him and Sarah.

Love.

With love you could make it through anything, Mrs.

Lewis had said. He had everything he could ever want in a woman with Sarah, except that. Except love.

And that thought didn't sit well.

Sarah was crawling along the floor taking measurements in the reception area of Wagner, McDuffy and Chambers. She'd sketched out her plans for the room and received Leland's approval. She was itching to start putting it all together.

The putting it together was her favorite part. Looking at a room, planning a new style and seeing it come to fruition…it was the wonder of her job.

She caught movement out of the corner of her eye and looked up. She watched as an old woman came down the staircase with a brown grocery bag.

"Who's that?" she asked Amelia after the woman had left.

"Oh, that's Mrs. Lewis. She's why you're lunching with me. She comes in to see Donovan every Wednesday at lunch always about changing her will."

"I don't think you're supposed to talk about that. Attorney-client privilege and all that." Maybe Mrs. Lewis is why he canceled that Wednesday lunch with her. He'd never really explained, and she'd never asked.

"Oh, there's no privilege. She'll tell anyone who will listen. And that's just what Donovan does… listens. She cuts people out, adds people back, and Donovan just listens. I don't think they ever really alter the thing, she just talks about it. She says we're her weekly therapy.''

"That's nice of Donovan.'' Darn. There were so many nice things about Donovan, and her mental list of them was rapidly going from full to overflowing.

Despite his messy office, he kept his home neat. He cooked divinely. He pitched in and helped with the cleanup. He was nice to old ladies. She'd never seen him kick a dog.

She almost wished he would. It would give her some reason to stay emotionally distant.

If he were truly The Iceman, it would be easy to ignore the twinges of…well, whatever it was she was feeling toward him. No, he wasn't The Iceman at all—he was sweet. She smiled as she thought about the description and how he'd react to hearing it. He wouldn't like it at all. Since that night he'd kissed her, he hadn't made any more physical moves in her direction. That was definitely sweet, and nice.

Darned nice, she thought as she let the tape measure *thwap* back full speed, making a satisfying noise.

Yeah. She was overjoyed he hadn't so much as grazed elbows with her since that night.

They came home at night, ate dinner together, shared bits and pieces of their day and then most nights they worked and maybe watched a television show together in chairs, separate and not touching.

Which is just what Sarah wanted. She assured herself of that fact a hundred times a day.

"You know," Amelia said, "Donovan's been different since you and him got engaged. He's...I don't know, more open. You're good for him. And I think he's good for you. You smile more."

Sarah stood up and maneuvered the ladder closer to a doorway. She wanted to measure the transom above the door. The small window had a crack in its glass. She wanted to see if she could replace it.

She'd spent so many hours planning this reception area and wanted everything perfect, including the glass. It was antique and had a lovely wavy quality to it. She knew a guy who might be able to find an antique replacement.

She climbed up toward the top so she could reach the glass.

"Hey, good-looking. Need a hand?" She looked down at Larry Mackenzie, a colleague of Donovan's she knew went by Mac and who'd generously offered to bring her back some lunch.

He hadn't been quite so generous with Amelia. As a matter of fact, his offer had been quite grudgingly made, and even more grudgingly accepted. When Sarah asked Amelia what was up, the normally gregarious receptionist had been strangely silent on the matter.

Sarah planned on finding out more later. For right now, she'd settle for her tacos.

Sarah looked down at the sandy-haired man who

stood at the base of the ladder. "Thanks, but I've got everything under control."

"Well, hurry up, lunch is getting cold."

"Just give me a minute," she said.

"What she's saying, Mackenzie, is go crawl back under your rock," Amelia said, in a very un-Amelia-like tone. "That is, after you hand over our lunch."

"Don't listen to her, sweetheart," Mac, ignoring Amelia, said to Sarah. "How about you dump that Donovan character you've hooked up with, and let me show you what a real man can offer you?"

"And who would that real man be, Mac?" Amelia asked sweetly. "Other than tacos, I haven't seen evidence that you have anything at all to offer a woman."

"Besides, where would you find a better man than Donovan?" Sarah asked saucily from the top rung of the ladder.

"You're looking at him," Mac said.

Amelia snorted.

Sarah grinned at the man, realizing this was more for Amelia's benefit than hers. "Oh, Mr. Mackenzie—"

"Mac," he corrected.

"Mac," she said obligingly as she double-checked the glass size. "You are definitely a real man, but I'm afraid Donovan got to me first. But if I'm ever available, I'll be sure to look you up."

"That's the way of the world. You use a man for

his tacos, then dash the rest of his hopes to the ground.''

Mac held one of the bags out in front of him. ''I guess I'll just have to satisfy myself with a delicious chicken soft taco. They've always been my favorites, no matter what their current incarnation. There have been so many changes over the years, but I feel as if I've changed with them. Matured, if you will. Why, once upon a time, a rejection like yours would have floored me.''

''Really?'' Sarah laughed at his melodramatic production.

''Ode to the taco…yeah, that's about your speed, Mackenzie,'' Amelia grumbled.

Sarah started to climb down from the ladder and he held out a hand. ''Here, allow me at least to save you from falling. If I can't win your heart, I'll just satisfy myself with saving your neck. It is such a lovely one, after all.''

''Oh, brother,'' Amelia groaned.

Sarah was just reaching for Mac's hand when Donovan practically barked, ''What are you doing?''

''Hi, honey,'' Sarah said, proud she'd remembered to use an endearment in front of his colleagues. She watched her fake fiancé rush down the stairs. ''I was just measuring this glass and getting ready for a lunch break.''

She'd asked him about having lunch together today, just as a means of reinforcing their charade to his colleagues, she'd assured herself. But he'd had an appointment, he'd said. Hence her acceptance of Mac's taco run.

"Speaking of breaking, do you want to break your neck?" Donovan yelled. "Get off the ladder, Sarah."

"I was here to catch her if she fell, Donovan," Mac said, his hand still extended.

"The taco-lover was trying to pick her up," Amelia grumbled.

"Just offering a helping hand," Mac said.

Donovan's face darkened. "Keep your hands off my fiancée."

"Why Donovan, that almost sounded like jealousy," Mac said, obviously unaware of Donovan's mounting annoyance. "The Iceman jealous? We might have to reassess your nickname."

"I'm all for helping you reassess. Let's start with the habit you have of flirting with the wrong women." Donovan elbowed Mac out of the way, and offered his hand to Sarah.

"Never the wrong ones. I only pick the oh-so-right ones, and your fiancée definitely qualifies except for her one small case of bad judgment in picking you over me."

"Sarah, come down," Donovan said.

Sarah ignored his extended hand and started down the ladder. "Don't speak to me as if I'm some lowly underling you can order about. I'm perfectly capable of climbing a ladder."

"It's not the climbing that scares me, it's the falling." His hand was now resting on her back, bracing her against the ladder so she could barely climb the rungs, much less fall.

"I'm a big girl, Donovan," she said.

What was with this me-Tarzan, you-Jane routine?

Because it had to be a routine. Just another facet to their ongoing charade. Donovan wasn't really jealous, although he was sounding as if he were. But he was just giving an award-winning performance. She could almost believe he was jealous.

Sarah finally had both feet firmly on the floor and turned to face Donovan. "I've been climbing ladders for years, and I was quite capable of dealing with this one."

"You're my fiancée, and it's my job to protect you."

"Protect me? Is that what you call it?" He might be acting, but she wasn't. This new caveman routine was annoying.

"Yes. What would you call it?"

"Being an overbearing jack—"

"Uh, uh, uh," Mac said. "I see my work is done, chaos is restored. I think I'll just leave your tacos here and go eat my scrumptious chicken soft taco in the quiet refuge of my own office. There I'll contemplate how all of life is represented in its soft flour shell and perfectly seasoned chicken and—"

"Oh, go soak your head, Mackenzie," Amelia said.

"Come with me," Donovan said, pulling Sarah along after him up the stairs and toward his office.

"Stop manhandling me."

"We need to talk."

"I'll say we do. But not until I've eaten." She grabbed at the bag. "I'm starving, and you need to settle down. I'm having lunch with Amelia and you? Well, you can—"

"Fine. I have an appointment anyway," he interrupted. "We'll talk tonight."

"Fine."

"And Sarah," he said softly—too softly.

"What?" she asked, aware of the fact Amelia was hanging on their every word.

"Stay away from Mac."

"You can't tell me what to do."

"I'm your fiancée, and I'll be your husband soon, so I have every right. You're not allowed to encourage other men."

"According to your definition, sharing tacos with a man constitutes encouraging?"

"It wasn't just tacos, he was flirting with you."

"To make Amelia jealous."

"Me?" Amelia squeaked. "Mac would never try to make me jealous. Crazy maybe, but not jealous."

Donovan laughed and talked right over Amelia saying, "You've got to be joking. Those two can't stand each other."

"See?" Amelia said. "Even Donovan knows we

can't stand each other. There's no way Mac would try to make me jealous by flirting with you.''

"That's what Mac wants you to think—that he doesn't like you. I think he's stuck in the playground mentality and trying to make you jealous because he does like you...a lot."

"Just stay away from him," Donovan said to Sarah. "If you want tacos, I'll buy you tacos. Hell, I'll make you tacos and once you've had my tacos you'll never want any other man's."

There was a suggestive lilt in his voice and she realized they weren't just talking about tacos.

"According to our agreement, I'm not going to have your tacos...ever."

"Maybe you could if you asked," he said.

"But I won't. I don't want your tacos and I never will." Okay, maybe that was a little lie. Donovan's tacos would be divine, she was sure.

"Donovan, you don't own me, and you can't boss me around," she said flatly. "And you can keep your tacos to yourself."

"We'll just see about that."

"Yeah. We will."

He stormed up the stairs, and Sarah could hear him muttering about tacos the entire way.

"Come on. Let's go find a quiet park bench and eat our tacos and you can explain what that was all about," Amelia said, practically pulling Sarah toward the door.

"You can't just leave your desk." She didn't want to explain anything to Amelia because she didn't understand any of it herself.

Tacos?

"It's lunch. There are no appointments for the next hour. Come on."

They crossed the street, Amelia still pulling Sarah with one hand and holding the taco bag with the other. She nodded at the first bench they came to.

"Talk," she demanded.

"There's nothing to talk about. We just had a little lover's spat. He was jealous of Mac."

"It was more than that. What was all that taco talk about?"

"Our lunch."

"Come on, Sarah, I thought we were friends, or at least at the cusp of being friends. We shared lunches, we shared stories, but you didn't share dating Donovan with me. But I understood that. I mean, he's a private man, and if he asked you to keep it quiet, I couldn't blame you. But there's something going on here. I'm not stupid."

Sarah weighed how much she could say without breaking the terms of her agreement with Donovan. "We're having some problems working out exactly what our relationship is. Obviously he sees it as a dictatorship with himself as the head-honcho. And I see it as a partnership, one that should be built on trust. How could he think I'd ever look at Larry Mackenzie? Oh, he's a nice enough man—"

Amelia scoffed, "Ha!"

"He is. But he's not Donovan." Sarah tore open a taco and took a bite.

"Boy, you've got it bad," Amelia said, following suit.

"Got what?" Sarah asked.

"Love. You're head-over-heels in love with him."

Sarah choked on a piece of lettuce. Love?

Yeah, right. But she couldn't say that to Amelia, so she settled for, "Maybe what's wrong, what's truly wrong, is I'm not sure how he feels about me."

"Oh, come on, Sarah, any fool with eyes can see how he feels. Do you think he'd come rushing in like that if he didn't care?"

"Maybe he was just protecting his interest."

"Or maybe he's as head over heels for you as you are for him."

Head over heels?

Is that what she was?

Head over heels for Elias Donovan?

Sarah wasn't sure. As a matter of fact, she hadn't felt sure about anything since this entire situation started. One minute, she'd been trying to build a business, and then next, she was engaged to be married to a man who didn't love her and she didn't love.

The last part, the *she didn't love* part, that didn't feel right. As a matter of fact, it felt distinctly wrong.

Love.

She couldn't be in love with Donovan, could she? After all, they hadn't known each other long enough.

"Sarah?" Amelia asked softly.

"What?"

"You do love Donovan, don't you?"

Love. Did she love him? Her head said no, but her heart cried out an entirely different answer. There wasn't even a fight. Her heart won out.

"Yes," Sarah said, her voice barely a whisper. "I guess I do. Loving Donovan changes everything."

"Yeah, love does that."

Sarah Jane Madison loved Elias Augustus Donovan, the man she was engaged to marry.

And loving him changed everything.

Chapter Nine

"Sarah?" Donovan called as he opened the door that evening.

Sarah knew he'd be home, but she hadn't thought it would be so soon.

She turned from the sauce she'd been stirring. "Dinner's almost done."

"You're cooking?"

"Yes." She'd wanted—no, needed—to do something. This was all she could think of. "I know you've done most of it, but I can cook. As a matter of fact, my spaghetti sauce generally garners all kinds of compliments."

"It smells good."

There was an awkward silence that enveloped the kitchen. Sarah turned back to stirring her sauce. Stirring was easier than facing Donovan. She knew what she had to do, and she knew why she had to do it, but she wasn't looking forward to it. As a matter of fact, she was pretty sure she was breaking her own heart.

"Why don't you go change?" Sarah said without turning around and looking at him.

"Fine." She heard the heels of his shoes tap against the tile floor, then stop. "Sarah?"

"Yes?" She studied the sauce, wondering if she'd put too much parsley in it. It had an awful lot of green flakes.

"I need to apologize about today."

"No, you don't, but we do need to talk." All those green flakes, she mused.

She was bound to get one stuck in her teeth. She had this dinner totally planned out, and didn't think green teeth would enhance any of her plans.

She didn't have to turn around to know he was still standing there, waiting expectantly. It was easier to worry about parsley than Donovan.

"All right," he finally said. "Let's talk."

"No. Not now. Later." She was giving them both one last dinner, then she'd do what had to be done. She'd do it because she loved him. "Go change, then we'll eat, and then we'll talk."

"If that's what you want."

"It's what I want."

What she wanted? That was a lie. None of this was

what she wanted. What she needed? Maybe. But what she wanted was…

No, she wasn't going to think about her fantasies. They were just that, flights of imagination that had no bearing whatsoever on the real world.

She'd planned this meal with as much care as Donovan had planned their engagement meal.

Oh, she wasn't taking him on a romantic dinner cruise, but she'd made a lovely meal, opened a bottle of wine, and planned to eat al fresco on the deck. She wanted the end of their relationship to be as pleasant as the beginning. Maybe that was odd, but there it was.

By the time he'd showered and changed, she had the table set and was just taking the spaghetti out. The wine was ice cold, and her heart was as well. But she welcomed the icy quiet of her heart. When the numbness wore off, she knew she'd be in a world of pain.

"About today," Donovan said, after he'd slid into his chair.

"No," she said. She knew what had to be done, but she was going to put it off for as long as she could. "Try my spaghetti first."

She served him and waited. He took the first bite and said, "You're right, you make a mean sauce. That's delicious."

"I add wine to the sauce. It helps." Such a mundane thing to say. What she wanted to say, to shout, was *I love you, you fool. I want to marry you in the truest sense of the word. I want to live with you and love you for the rest of my life.*

But he didn't feel that way. To him she was just business. She couldn't go through with a marriage-of-convenience, because loving him would make that type of marriage not just inconvenient, but painful. She'd rather break her own heart tonight, just this once, rather than break it day after day. And that's what would happen if she lived with a man who didn't share her feelings.

He was still eating her spaghetti, unaware of her inner turmoil.

"And did you make the meatballs?" he asked as he finished another bite.

"Yep. The entire thing is from scratch."

"I'm impressed."

"I'm glad." It was as if they'd used up all their small talk. They both made a show of eating their meal, though it tasted like sawdust in her mouth.

She stared at the bay. It was easier than looking at Donovan.

She loved him.

She wasn't sure when it had happened. She wasn't even sure why it happened, because she hadn't been looking to fall in love. But she had.

She twirled the engagement ring around her finger. In a few minutes it would be off her hand and back in Donovan's possession. Someday he'd find a woman he loved, and that woman would wear the ring. That someday-woman would be the one to go to Ireland with him and fulfill his grandmother's wish.

"Sarah, I just want to apologize about today," Donovan said, interrupting her musings.

"There's no need. I just need you to know that I truly wasn't flirting with Mac. I wouldn't do that to you," she replied.

"I know. I don't have any explanation for the way I behaved. All I can do is apologize."

She'd thought about how to do this all afternoon. She knew Donovan wouldn't simply let her walk away without a fight. He needed her…at least he needed to be married. Any woman would do. So, rather than just telling him it was over, she'd come up with another plan.

"We have to talk about this marriage," she said. "It's just around the corner, and we still haven't totally worked out the prenuptial agreement. I think today is a perfect example of why we need one. We need everything, absolutely everything, nailed down."

"I've been making notes since we started."

"So have I." She reached into her jean's pockets and pulled out her paper. "I've started making a list of everything we've discussed. I know I'm not a lawyer, but I think they're pretty clear and basic."

Taking a deep breath, she began, "Item one— What's yours now remains yours after the marriage is dissolved. What's mine now remains mine, as well.''

"I think that just about covers everything," Donovan said.

"Oh, no," she said. "You originally said we needed to pin down *everything,* and I think we need more than just that one basic term. Item two— There will be no mutual purchases. If an item breaks and needs to be replaced, one party will purchase the replacement, and retain ownership after the marriage dissolves.

"Item three—"

"Sarah, I don't think we need to go through this point by point," he said, exasperation in his voice.

"Oh, but we do," she assured him, and rattled off everything they'd already agreed to, and then began the new things. "Item twenty-eight. Donovan will take out the garbage. If he will not be home early enough to get the garbage out he must verbally inform Sarah that she will need to do the job."

"Sarah, there is no way that needs to be in the prenup. It's common sense that if I can't do it, you will." This time there was more than a little exasperation in his voice; there was a ton.

She'd planned on picking a fight, and it was working. The thought gave her no satisfaction, though.

"No, it's not," she argued. "You said we needed everything written down. And I want everything."

"I didn't mean we had to include my willingness

to go to dinner at your parents once a week when they get home from Europe.''

''They'll want to get to know you,'' she said.

''Sarah, all you'd have to do is ask and I'd come.''

''But you're the one who insisted we put everything down. It's not as if we love each other, and have the trust that accompanies that.'' Saying the words broke her heart just a little more.

She forced herself to continue. ''We've become friends, or at least I'd thought so until right now, but still, you were right. It should all be in writing.''

''Even the part about my putting my dirty clothes in the hamper?'' he asked.

''I tripped over your towel.''

''It was in my bathroom.''

''Which I was cleaning. Bathrooms are my job,'' she said.

''Another little prenup condition. What item number was that?''

''Seventeen, I think. Do you want me to check?''

''No. I don't think you need to put household tasks in the agreement.''

''Well, you're doing the vacuuming and dusting and cooking, and we're splitting the kitchen cleanup, so it stands to reason that—''

''I don't want to be reasonable, and I'm tired of putting all these clauses and conditions in what was supposed to be a simple prenuptial agreement.'' He drained his wine and set the glass down with enough force that Sarah jumped.

"Don't you see, there's nothing simple about this situation." That's what her new absurd terms were supposed to show. He didn't realize how truly complex this had become…at least for her. Marrying a man she loved, a man who didn't love her—it didn't get more complex than that.

"It could be simple if you'd let it."

"Maybe I don't want to let it," she said. "Maybe I don't want it to be simple. Maybe I feel that a marriage should be work. And if the only work I can make you do is a prenup, well then there it is."

"I don't understand you," he said, his tone harsh and hard.

"I know," she said sadly. And she wasn't about to explain it all to him.

"Fine. You want to add new terms? Nit-picky little terms? Then let's address what happened with Mackenzie today. I want to add a condition to the prenup. No flirting with other men."

"I wasn't flirting," she said. "He was using me to make Amelia jealous."

"No way. Those two can't stand each other."

"You said that before, and you were wrong before. That's what they'd both like you to think."

"You're crazy and you're changing the subject. I'm adding that term."

"Fine. But I'm not done with my terms. Item number, oh, I don't know what number it is, but every Tuesday we eat at Taco Bell.''

"What?" he asked, his pen frozen. "You're putting Taco Bell into a prenup? Sarah, that's absurd.''

"And Christmases," she said, ignoring his argument, and ignoring the pain that was growing so strong in her chest that she thought her heart might just explode. "We haven't talked about where to spend the holidays.''

"I'm not dividing our holidays between my family and yours in a prenup.''

"And Disney World," she said, still ignoring him. "I want to go. In the fall. You're not writing. Start writing. In the fall. Late September's a slow time. We'll stay at the Polynesian of course.''

"Sarah, I'm not writing all this down." He tossed the pad and pen down into the middle of the table and folded his arms over his chest. "This is over.''

"And I want you to write down that you'll never drink so much you'd lose your leg. That even if you did, I'd never use that as a reason to leave. That—''

She realized she was crying. That was the last thing she wanted to do.

"What is this all about?" he asked, his voice suddenly softer.

"I can't do it, Donovan. I'm so sorry." Tears were rolling down her cheeks, but she simply let them fall and concentrated on getting the words out. "I really thought I could. But I can't. I was picking a fight, but

I don't want to end this way. It seemed like a good idea this afternoon, but not now. I just can't marry you. Blame it on me. Tell everyone you tried—which you did—but I was unreasonable. Which I was. I already packed up my clothes.''

"You already packed?" he asked. "What was this, your way of illustrating a point? If so, I don't get it.''

"I...I have to go. That's the only point you need to get.''

"Sarah.''

"Listen, Donovan, we can't even agree on what we're putting in a prenuptial agreement. How on earth do you expect us to be able to agree on anything in the marriage?''

"It's not the same.''

"It is. Essentially we're strangers.''

"Strangers? You've been living with me for almost a month. I know things about you. I know you cry when you watch old movies, and that Back Street is your favorite. I know you like your wine ice-cold, not just chilled. I know you have a fondness for sunsets, and for seagulls, despite the fact they're nothing more than flying rats.''

"They're beautiful," she whispered.

"I know you love your family. I know you're independent and determined. I know that you're a wonderful decorator, and because of that I know that By Design will prosper and flourish.''

"Thanks to you and the introductions you've made.

But all that aside, and no matter how grateful I am for everything you've done for me, I don't think this is going to work. You do know a lot about me, but there are still things you don't know, and I don't think you'll ever know."

"You could teach me."

She shook her head, sadly. "No. There are things you can't teach. And I've learned enough about you to know that you're not someone who likes to be told things. When Leland told you that you needed to balance your life, you bristled."

"I have a plan. It's not as if I plan to make work the center of my life forever. It's just that my parents taught me that a career and a family don't mix. I want to wait until my career is solid and I can cut back on work before I commit to a family."

"When will it be solid enough, Donovan?" Sarah sighed. "I know you've got your life all figured out. And I'm not really a part of that plan. I'm just a detour you're taking until you can get on with what it is you really want. And Donovan, I've discovered I can't be a detour."

Her heart was breaking. She swore she could feel it severing within her chest. Could a person bleed to death because of a broken heart? She was about to find out because she had to finish the job.

"I'm leaving," she said.

"I don't want you to go."

"But I have to. If I stay, if I were to do this, we'd end up hating each other."

"I could never hate you."

"That's what you say, but you could. You would. I'm packed and I'm going."

"Sarah, please don't go."

She leaned down and kissed him. "I'm sorry."

She dropped the ring on the table.

The sound echoed in her mind as she walked out the door.

Chapter Ten

The next evening Sarah massaged her aching shoulder. She wasn't looking forward to trying to sleep on her sleeper-sofa again tonight. The boulder had grown while she was away and one night sleeping on it was more than enough.

But the lump in the middle of the bed wasn't nearly as big as the unexpected lump that formed in her throat when she started the fight with Donovan last night. That lump in her throat had sunk and stuck somewhere around the fragments of her heart.

She'd been engaged to a man she hardly knew, then was stupid enough to fall in love with him.

Oh, how dumb could a girl get?

Not much dumber.

What was she going to do now?

Pick up and get on with her life. She had a business to build, and…

Well, she'd learned her lesson from Donovan. She was going to forget everything else, and focus on what mattered…her career.

She could control her business, but it seemed she couldn't control her heart. It had a mind of its own, and it had decided on Donovan.

There was a loud thump at the door.

Sarah put her head under the pillow. It wasn't even seven o'clock yet. And that meant whoever was at the door wasn't a client or potential client, so she didn't have to answer it.

But the thumping continued and escalated in volume.

Grumbling, she got out of bed, tossed a sweatshirt on over the T-shirt and sweats she'd worn to bed, and got the door.

"Pearly? What's up?" she asked with a yawn.

"What are you doing here, and not at home?"

"This is my home," Sarah said.

Pearly pushed past her into the room. "You live with Donovan."

"Lived with. Past tense." Sarah let the door thump closed.

"So, you didn't pay any attention to poor Lerlene's lesson, did you?"

"No. I paid attention to you. You're happy in your

singleness, and I'm sure I will be, too. It just gives me more time to focus on my business."

"Hmm, that's what you say, but for some reason, I don't believe you."

"Pearly, I don't want to be rude, but it doesn't matter what you believe. I believe it. Breaking up with Donovan was for the best."

"Okay. If you say so."

"I do. I mean, he didn't love me. They call him The Iceman, and with good reason. His heart is frozen solid and I couldn't thaw it."

"He looked rather hot-blooded when he was around you." Pearly just stared at her, studying her. Looking for something.

Sarah wasn't sure what the older woman was look-ing for, and she didn't care. "What you saw in Donovan's eyes was lust. I want more than that. I want—"

"What do you want, Sarah?"

"Love. I wanted love, and that was the one thing he couldn't give me."

She started to cry. She'd sworn she wouldn't, but she did. Pearly wrapped her arms around her, and Sarah allowed her friend to hold her tight.

She stood in the middle of By Design being held by Pearly as she sobbed.

"Are you sure? About Donovan's feelings?" Pearly asked.

"Sure, I'm sure. He's never said he loved me."

"Ah, but has he showed you? Has he put your feelings first, tried to make you happy?"

"Well, yes."

"And I'll attest to the fact that when the two of you were in a room together, you were the only woman he saw."

Sarah scoffed.

"Truly. And Amelia told me about his little jealous temper tantrum over Mac and tacos."

"He wasn't jealous."

"No? Then what was that?"

"We had a deal…part of the prenup. No flirting with other people."

"According to Amelia, you weren't flirting with Mac, he was flirting with you."

"No. He was trying to make her jealous."

"There's that, too," Pearly said with a laugh. "Don't think we haven't noticed it. But he was doing it by flirting with you. Why would that bother Donovan if he didn't care?"

Sarah pulled back and sniffed. "Donovan was just…"

"Just?"

"Oh, I don't know. But I know he doesn't love me."

"Did I ever tell you about the big library fine I got last year?"

"Library fine?" Oh, gosh, here it came…another Pearly story.

"Yeah, I'd borrowed *War and Peace* and told myself it was time to get some culture. Well, six months later, it was still sitting on my nightstand, gathering dust. Every night, I started it, and every night I ended up with a romance in my hand instead. I love romances. I love that two people learn to look past the masks we all wear and see what's really inside. If I thought you'd looked past Donovan's, I'd shut up. But I don't think you have."

"Pearly, let me guarantee you that even if I peeled back his mask, all I'd find is a man who's focused on his career. I was just another stepping-stone."

"Did you ever tell him how you felt?" Pearly asked.

"No. He didn't want to talk about things like feelings. He wanted to talk about business and prenups. That's what we talked about."

"Listen, I paid my library fine, and admitted that I know what I like. It's not what's good for me, it's what feels right. You're afraid to admit to yourself Donovan's right for you."

"That's not the question. The question is, am I right for him?" Tears started to flow again as she admitted, "And the answer's no."

"Girl, you got me so flubbergusted—"

"Flubbergusted?"

"Shh. You've got me so riled I can't even think of a story. Don't tell Josie, she'd never let me live it down. I'm leaving, but I'm going to tell you that love is too precious to let it slip through your fingers.''

"Like Lerlene and Trubald.''

''No, like you and Donovan. You're both afraid to tell the other what you're feeling.''

Donovan was going to win Sarah back.

This was it, he thought as he fingered the ring— her ring—that sat in front of him on his desk.

He'd argued any number of cases, and won a huge percentage, but he'd never been so terrified of losing a fight.

Because he didn't know what he'd do without Sarah. Somehow he was going to make her see that marrying him was to her advantage. And once he had that ring on her finger, he was going to romance her into loving him.

When she'd left, he'd sat on the deck and didn't worry at all about his promotion. Hell, he didn't care if he made partner. It didn't matter. What mattered was Sarah. Her leaving had left a hole in his heart, and he knew he'd never fill it without her. He needed her.

She was a part of him.

In those few short weeks, she'd fit neatly into his life, filling up parts he'd never realized were empty, until she'd come along. He was aching with the emptiness now that she was gone.

He wanted her back. Not because it made sense business-wise, but because…

He loved her.

It was that simple.

He loved Sarah. Maybe he'd loved her right from the start. Maybe that's why asking her to marry him hadn't just seemed prudent, but had seemed right.

She was right for him.

And he was right for her.

She might not know it yet, but she would.

He had a few plans to make, and then he was going to catch his wife.

He put the ring in his pocket, ready to go find the woman he loved. Before he could get up, the door opened. Sarah burst into the house.

"Do you still want to marry me?" she asked without preamble.

"Yes. I—"

"If you do, there's just one more term for the prenup."

"What else do you want?" he asked. "Steak every Monday night? A movie every Saturday night? The beach, the dock, the moon? Tell me. I'll get it for you, do it for you. Just tell me."

"There's only one other thing I'd want. One more term—a term that would negate the need for any of the others. But some things are beyond even your power. It's something you can't force, you can't buy. And I'm so afraid it's something you can't give me, but Pearly convinced me I had to come and ask. To just let this end without even trying...that would haunt me.''

''Ask me. I'll give it to you if I can. There's so much I want to give you.''

She walked up and leaned over his desk, her face, her lovely face, just inches from his. ''And there's only one thing I want from you. Love. Donovan, I need you to love me. You can feed me all the logical reasons why we should marry, but in the end, there's only one reason I could marry you, and it's the one thing you can't give me.''

''Here,'' he said, pulling an envelope from a pile of papers on his desk and handing it to her. ''I was coming to find you after I took care of this. Look in the envelope, Sarah.''

She opened the envelope and saw tickets and brochures.

''What's this?''

''Tickets for our honeymoon.''

''We never discussed a honeymoon. It wouldn't make sense. I have too much work to do here building my business, and you have to build your practice.''

He stood and walked around his desk, standing right in front of the woman he loved. ''Yes, we both have things to do. I have a partnership to achieve, and you have a business to build. But none of that matters to me. You see, more than any of that, we have to build our love, give it time to take root and flourish.

The tickets, they're to Ireland. I promised my grand-mother someday a Donovan bride would wear that ring, this ring...."

He took her hand in his and slipped her ring back on her finger and prayed she never took it off again. "I promised my grandmother a woman I loved would wear this ring to Ireland and fulfill that promise made so many years ago by another Donovan."

"But—"

"Sarah, listen, I think I fell in love with you that first day."

"When I came into your office and asked you to sue the Rat?"

"No. Before that. When it was raining and I stum-bled into your store. You...there was something there. Some undescribable spark. I didn't know what it was, didn't want to know. Yet, after that, I couldn't seem to get away from you. I saw you eating in the park, talking to Amelia, feeding pigeons."

He couldn't even describe the force of that feeling to her adequately. He'd hidden from it for so long, but couldn't any longer. It was love, but not just any love. It was the type of love Leland had for his wife, the type his grandmother and grandfather had shared.

"Do you think I would have asked just any woman to pretend to be my fiancée?" he asked softly.

"Yes," she said with a strangled laugh that quickly turned to tears.

"Don't cry, sweetheart. I love you. I'll put it in the

prenup along with anything else. But to be honest, we don't need one, because if you agree to marry me, there's no way I'm ever letting you go.''

"Donovan, we haven't known each other long enough." Sarah had come in here ready to fight for just this, and yet, here he was, offering her her dream, his love, and for a moment there was fear. But as she looked into his eyes, the fear was replaced by something stronger, something big enough to overcome anything, even fear.

"Say you love me," he said, his hand stroking her cheek.

"Elias…"

"I love the way my name sounds on your lips. Say it again."

"Elias. I love you. Only you. I've known it for a long time. It just took me a while to admit it to myself."

"And when you did, you broke off the engagement?" he asked.

"Something like that."

"So you'll marry me?"

All her fears and tears were gone. She laughed. "Well, Mrs. Wagner and the girls have put a lot of work into that wedding. It would be rude to spoil their fun."

"Yes, that would be one reason," he said, his laughter echoing her own.

"And our marrying would be good for business,"

she said, stepping closer, moving into the shelter of his arms and knowing she'd never move far from them again.

"Business doesn't matter," he said, pulling her close, encircling her, not just physically. No, she was surrounded by his love.

"Well, I guess I can think of one other reason why we should get married," she teased.

"What's that?"

"Because I can't live another day without you." She started chuckling. "You know, Pearly would love to tell this story."

"You know, I don't think anyone would believe this story if she told it," he said, his own laughter rumbling in his chest, sending little waves of desire coursing through Sarah's being.

"No, I guess this is a story that you and I will keep to ourselves...a love story unlike any other." So saying, she kissed him. Kissed the man she loved and knew that she'd truly found her home.

Epilogue

"How nice of Ratgaz to pay for supper last night," Sarah said. "Lucky for me I had a heck of an attorney."

"The best," Donovan teased. "The settlement was more than I'd thought we'd get and certainly paid for not just your expertise, but your aggravation, though I'd still have liked to punch the Rat out."

"Shh," she said softly. "I don't want to think about him. I only want to think happy thoughts. Nothing else is allowed here in this land of legends and fairy dreams."

They stood, hand in hand, in front of the Malahide Castle in Ireland. It was a towering old structure, surrounded by gardens and peacocks, and...

Love.

Sarah had discovered that no matter where she went, when Donovan was with her, she was surrounded by love.

The wedding was everything Mrs. Wagner and the girls had planned. Her parents had immediately fallen for her new husband; and his parents, though they were distant, seemed happy enough. And after Leland had announced Donovan's partnership at the reception, his parents had positively beamed.

"A penny for your thoughts," he said as they started walking into town.

"I don't think you get to use American money here, but I'll tell you my thoughts anyway.... I love you so much I could burst with it."

"And I love you, too, Sarah Jane Madison-Donovan. My grandmother would be pleased."

As they walked through the quaint little town down toward the beach, Sarah knew that this particular love story wasn't simply ending with a happily ever after.

No, it was the beginning of one.

* * * * *

Don't miss the 100th volume of
Harlequin Duets in May 2003,
which includes a brand-new title from
Holly Jacobs,
THE HUNDRED-YEAR ITCH.

SILHOUETTE *Romance*®

Coming in April 2003, look for brand-new stories from two of Silhouette Romance's brightest stars.

A beautiful image consultant makes every attempt to ignore her heart and turn one ruggedly handsome blue-collar bachelor into

A WHOLE NEW MAN
Roxann Delaney
(SR #1658)

Confident she's put her past behind her, a sophisticated city girl returns home and comes face-to-face with the love of her life. One look and she knows

HE'S STILL THE ONE
Cheryl Kushner
(SR #1659)

Available at your favorite retail outlet.

Silhouette®
Where love comes alive™

Visit Silhouette at www.eHarlequin.com   SRWNMHS

Coming in April 2003 from

SILHOUETTE *Romance*®

and

Judy Christenberry
DADDY ON THE DOORSTEP
(#1654)

He was rich, he was handsome...and Nicholas Avery was going to be a daddy! When Andrea Avery realized that her brief marriage to the business tycoon had resulted in a bundle of joy, her protective instincts told her to keep the child a secret. After all, the last thing Nick wanted was a family....

Or was it?

Available at your favorite retail outlet.

Silhouette®

Where love comes alive™

Visit Silhouette at www.eHarlequin.com   SRDOTD

If you enjoyed what you just read,
then we've got an offer you can't resist!

Take 2 bestselling love stories FREE!

Plus get a FREE surprise gift!

Clip this page and mail it to Silhouette Reader Service™

IN U.S.A.	**IN CANADA**
3010 Walden Ave.	P.O. Box 609
P.O. Box 1867	Fort Erie, Ontario
Buffalo, N.Y. 14240-1867	L2A 5X3

YES! Please send me 2 free Silhouette Romance® novels and my free surprise gift. After receiving them, if I don't wish to receive anymore, I can return the shipping statement marked cancel. If I don't cancel, I will receive 6 brand-new novels every month, before they're available in stores! In the U.S.A., bill me at the bargain price of $3.34 plus 25¢ shipping and handling per book and applicable sales tax, if any*. In Canada, bill me at the bargain price of $3.80 plus 25¢ shipping and handling per book and applicable taxes**. That's the complete price and a savings of at least 10% off the cover prices—what a great deal! I understand that accepting the 2 free books and gift places me under no obligation ever to buy any books. I can always return a shipment and cancel at any time. Even if I never buy another book from Silhouette, the 2 free books and gift are mine to keep forever.

215 SDN DNUM
315 SDN DNUN

Name	(PLEASE PRINT)	
Address	Apt.#	
City	State/Prov.	Zip/Postal Code

* Terms and prices subject to change without notice. Sales tax applicable in N.Y.
** Canadian residents will be charged applicable provincial taxes and GST.
   All orders subject to approval. Offer limited to one per household and not valid to current Silhouette Romance® subscribers.
   ® are registered trademarks of Harlequin Books S.A., used under license.

SROM02   ©1998 Harlequin Enterprises Limited

Silhouette Romance presents tales of
enchanted love and things beyond explanation
in the heartwarming series,

Soulmates

Couples destined for each other are brought
together by the powerful magic of love....

The second time around
brings an unexpected suitor, in
THE WISH
by Diane Pershing (on sale April 2003)

The power of love battles a medieval spell, in
THE KNIGHT'S KISS
by Nicole Burnham (on sale May 2003)

Soulmates

Some things are meant to be....

*Available at
your favorite retail outlet.*

Silhouette®

Where love comes alive™

Visit Silhouette at www.eHarlequin.com   SRSOUL4

eHARLEQUIN.com

Sit back, relax and enhance your romance
with our great magazine reading!

- **Sex and Romance!** Like your romance
  hot? Then you'll *love* the sensual reading
  in this area.

- **Quizzes!** Curious about your lovestyle?
  His commitment to you? Get the
  answers here!

- **Romantic Guides and Features!**
  Unravel the mysteries of love with
  informative articles and advice!

- **Fun Games!** Play to your heart's content....

**Plus...romantic recipes,
top ten lists,
Lovescopes...and more!**

**Enjoy our online magazine today—
visit www.eHarlequin.com!**

INTMAG

Secrets and passion abound
as the royals reclaim their throne!

Bestselling author

RAYE MORGAN

brings you a special installment
of her new miniseries

ROYAL NIGHTS

On sale May 2003

When a terrifying act of sabotage nearly takes the life of Prince Damian
of Nabotavia, he is plunged into a world of darkness. Hell-bent on
discovering who tried to kill him, the battle-scarred prince searches
tirelessly for the truth. The unwavering support of Sara, his fearless
therapist, is the only light in Damian's bleak world. But will revealing
his most closely guarded secret throw Sara into the line of fire?

Don't miss the other books in this exciting miniseries:

JACK AND THE PRINCESS (Silhouette Romance #1655)
On sale April 2003

BETROTHED TO THE PRINCE (Silhouette Romance #1667)
On sale June 2003

COUNTERFEIT PRINCESS (Silhouette Romance #1672)
On sale July 2003

Available wherever Silhouette books are sold.

Where love comes alive™

Visit Silhouette at www.eHarlequin.com   PSRN

SILHOUETTE *Romance*®

introduces regal tales of love and honor in the exciting new miniseries

CATCHING
THE
CROWN

by Raye Morgan

When the Royal Family of Nabotavia is called to return to
its native land after years of exile, the princes and
princesses must do their duty. But will they meet their
perfect match before it's too late?

Find out in:

JACK AND THE PRINCESS (#1655)
On sale April 2003

BETROTHED TO THE PRINCE (#1667)
On sale June 2003

and

COUNTERFEIT PRINCESS (#1672)
On sale July 2003

And don't miss the exciting story of Prince Damian of Nabotavia in

ROYAL NIGHTS

*Coming in May 2003, a special Single Title found
wherever Silhouette books are sold.*

**Available at your favorite retail outlet.
Only from Silhouette Books!**

Silhouette®

Where love comes alive™

Visit Silhouette at www.eHarlequin.com   SRCTCR

SILHOUETTE Romance

COMING NEXT MONTH

SRCNM0303